Everyday Warriors

by

Ruth Hunter

Turtle Press   **Hartford**

EVERYDAY WARRIORS

Copyright © 2000 Ruth Hunter. All rights reserved. Printed in the United States of America. No part of this book may be reproduced without written permission except in the case of brief quotations embodied in articles or reviews. For information, address Turtle Press, PO Box 290206, Wethersfield CT 06129-0206.

Photographs used with permission from the principles.

To contact the author, any of the stars who participated in this book or to order additional copies of this book:
Turtle Press
401 Silas Deane Hwy
P.O. Box 290206
Wethersfield, CT 06129-0206
1-880-77-TURTL

Turtle Press will make every effort to forward your correspondence to the martial arts stars featured in this book.

ISBN 1-880336-30-8

Front Cover photos:
Top row: (l-r) Katelyn Sleznikow, Emily Roeske, Benny "The Jet" Urquidez, Sang H. Kim, Jason David Frank
Bottom row: (l-r) Howard Jackson, Bob Wall, Cynthia Rothrock, Pat Burleson, Christine Bannon-Rodrigues

Back Cover photos:
(clockwise from top) Joe Lewis, J. P. Roeske, Kathy Long, Juan Moreno, Bill "Superfoot" Wallace, Bryan Paris

Dedication:

To my parents Jim and Margaret Lightner; my mother-in-law Elsie (Gwen) Hunter; and my sister-in-law Jenny Lightner for their faith in me.

Acknowledgment

I would like to thank all of the people who appear in this book. They believed in and supported this project, willingly sharing their stories with me and connecting me with others. Their experiences in the martial arts have led them to conduct their lives in ways that express martial arts philosophies in action.

Ruth Hunter

Note to Parents and Instructors:

Children learn in many different ways, but one of the most effective is through stories.

Hearing about other people's experiences serves at least two purposes which increase the likelihood of long-term involvement with the martial arts. One is that stories describe how people apply their martial arts training in everyday life. This helps broaden their understanding of how what they are learning applies to everyday living.

The other is that it communicates that children have a common bond with all other martial artists. Children are often surprised and inspired to learn that their heroes feel the same emotions they feel including fear, sadness, anger, and excitement. The sense that they are part of something larger than themselves provides an essential sense of belonging.

The stories are grouped according to reading levels, with Level One being the most easily read or understood and Level Three the most challenging. Level One stories deal with concepts that should be familiar to young martial artists in preschool through first grade. The concepts put forth are simple to understand and the stories shorter in length. Level Two stories are most appropriate for children in grades two through four, although they can be enjoyed by children of all ages with some help from an adult.

Level Three stories deal with abstract concepts or more mature story matter faced by children in upper elementary and middle grades like saying no to alcohol, drugs or smoking. When your child is ready, these stories can be valuable springboards for more serious discussions about these important issues.

As children's reading abilities grow, they will find more stories to relate to and learn from. In addition, you can actively share all of the stories with your children and students. Discuss the person's reaction in the story. Is it the way your young person thinks he or she would react? What are some other options? What are some of the consequences of reacting differently? Discuss the philosophies. For instance, what does "courtesy" mean? How did your young person use "courtesy" during the day? How did the other person respond? Making these stories a part of your life and classes, can help students realize the extent martial arts philosophies can affect their everyday lives.

What is an Everyday Warrior?

Years ago, when Justin was 12, and preparing for his Black Belt test, his father asked him exactly how much he had to know to be ready for his promotion.

"Everything," Justin replied.

"If you learn everything now, what will you have to learn after you get your Black Belt?"

"Everything else."

The study of martial arts goes beyond the ability to perform the physical movements. It's an understanding of the underlying philosophies and making them part of your life. It's developing self-respect and respect for others.

The martial artist learns that fighting is a last resort. The purpose is to win battles; fighting is easy. Winning is hard. Winning requires strategy, self-control and strength of character.

Understanding can come early in your growth, or it can come after several years of being a Black Belt.

Each of us is an Everyday Warrior, at different stages of our development. Every time we react to a situation with strategy, not just emotion, we win. Every time we keep our emotions in balance, we win. Every time we control our own actions and don't let what we do be decided by the actions of others, we win. Every time we keep our goals in front of us and continue to try to meet them, regardless of hard times or negative attitudes of others, we win. Every time we stick up for our friends, we win. Every time we stand up for our beliefs, for the rights of every human being, we win. Every time we keep our promises, we win. Every time we take responsibility for our actions instead of blaming others, we win.

Martial arts teaches people to take care of themselves. Once we learn the physical skills, we learn they are not our only choice. We learn to use our minds to handle situations. We must choose when to use our physical and mental skills and which ones to use.

When we have to fight to stop an attacker, our reactions must be made from a calm center. Our actions can't be based on revenge, on wanting to hurt someone. We only do what is necessary to stop an attack, not glory in violence.

Students studying the martial arts gain confidence. They carry themselves well. They no longer walk as if they expect to be hurt and attacked. They are no longer in "victim mode." This can be enough to keep would-be attackers away.

Each martial artist faces the "dangerous" ground, when physical skills are developed to the point where they can be used effectively, but mental skills aren't centered. Often the dangerous ground comes around the brown or red belt level. As one martial artist stated, "I felt like a shark in a pool of guppies." As the martial artist continued to study and grow mentally, the physical skills became a natural part of her and she regained her calm center.

True martial artists are those who have learned not to be victims and at the same time, not to be bullies.

The road to being an Everyday Warrior is not smooth. Sometimes we fail. The road is an ongoing process to make these philosophies part of ourselves and a way of life. We want these philosophies to be a part of us so that we automatically respond with winning attitudes and conduct.

If we spend too much time thinking about how we should react, our mind can get in the way of our reactions. Martial artists reach a point where physical and mental reactions come naturally, an outgrowth of all of their studies.

Becoming an Everyday Warrior is an ongoing process. It takes time to develop into our true selves. We will continue to evolve and grow throughout our lives. Our ultimate goal is to live a life based on philosophies such as integrity, honor, wisdom, humility, courtesy, discipline and self-control.

Martial artists need to be calm during a crisis. When we are calm, we can figure out what is going on and react to it, not to what we fear or imagine will happen. Our outward actions are the result of our inward thoughts.

Confronting our inner fears are all a part of the journey, our process of developing into Everyday Warriors.

It will take time. Change takes time. Our journey toward our goals starts with what we decide to do right at this moment. Remember that we can complete this journey if we take it action by action, thought by thought. Each person makes their own journey through life. Yours is an individual journey that begins with you.

The choices we face in our daily lives are rarely easy. Doing right can be hard. Our actions always result in consequences. As thinking martial artists in control of our own actions, we know what the consequences are before we act.

Concentration

    Concentration is the way to the controlled, calm center of yourself. It is focusing all of your efforts, energies and thoughts on doing one thing well. It could be anything: a math test, a tournament, doing homework or helping around the house.

    An Everyday Warrior divides the big task into smaller tasks. This makes it easier to concentrate on each aspect and succeed at the larger task, whether it is doing a better job or giving a better performance.

    Concentration involves the total body and mind. It is easier to concentrate when bodies and minds are relaxed and alert. Since breathing moves oxygen throughout the body, breathing properly helps the Everyday Warrior stay relaxed and alert. With oxygen, fingers, legs and minds work more quickly.

    Concentration helps you let go of fears, freeing you to deal with the current situation.

Christine Bannon-Rodrigues

Mrs. Bannon-Rodriques, who studies Kenpo Karate, is a champion in point fighting, weapons and forms. She acted as the stunt double for Hilary Swank in The Next Karate Kid *and for Alicia Silverstone who played Batgirl in* Batman and Robin. *Mrs. Bannon-Rodrigues starred as Lady Lightening in the TV series* WMAC Masters.

☯ At first, karate was simply an after-school activity, a way for my girlfriend and I to learn self-defense.

But then I became involved in the competitive aspect and the after-school activity became more than I had originally planned. My first tournament was one which my instructor promoted, and I took part mostly because the other students were. I really enjoyed competing, but I wasn't serious about it or outstanding. I actually just liked going away on weekends with the other students.

I was almost a Black Belt before I became a serious competitor. Back then, the only people rated in the magazines were the top ten Black Belts. I wanted to see my name in the magazine. I trained hard and made the top ten in New England and soon, I was ranked nationally. My self-confidence grew, and I raised my goals.

In 1990, I qualified for the first time for the World Championships which were to be held in Venice, Italy. But then my father suffered a stroke and was placed in the hospital. He was extremely ill. I didn't want to leave him and travel to Venice. I wanted to be near him, to be around in case he needed me.

My father, however, had other plans. He'd always been very proud of my martial arts accomplishments. He told me I should go to Venice and compete.

I went, but my mind wasn't centered on the upcoming competition. I continually worried about my father. The reports all said he wasn't doing well. But he had encouraged me to come, and if I didn't do my best, he would be disappointed. I wanted to justify his pride and faith in me.

During the forms competition, I concentrated. I was determined to block out my fears and do my absolute best. For those few minutes in front of the judges, I focused entirely on my form, putting everything I had into it. It was the same in the sparring ring. I concentrated totally on each opponent I faced.

I ended up winning the gold medal in forms and the bronze medal in fighting. I returned home in hopes to show my father my medals, share my success and feel his happiness and pride in me. However, when I returned he was in a coma. He died a few weeks later, but I knew I was doing what he wanted me to do.

I went on to become an 8-time world champion, winning gold medals in forms, fighting and weapons at three World Championships: Venice, Italy; London, England; and Atlantic City. ☯

Mrs. Bannon-Rodrigues was faced with a hard decision. She didn't want to leave her father when he was sick, but he wanted her to compete. She was worried about him, but in order to honor his belief in her abilities, she concentrated to do her best in every moment of the competition.

Katie Fisher

Katie is a purple belt.

I entered my first taekwondo tournament because I thought it would be fun to join my brother, Dad and Mom. I had seen Mom and Dad compete before and they looked like they were having a good time.

I felt kind of embarrassed because I'd never competed, but taekwondo taught me to not be afraid to try new things. I knew what to say to introduce my form and then I started it. I won first place in my division.

I was happy. I'm going to compete again as soon as I can. ☯

By concentrating and practicing the different parts of forms competition: entering the ring, announcing her form to the judges, her form and what to do when she was finished, Katie was prepared and did well.

Addison

Addison, 11, is a blue belt.

I play basketball on our school team. At our last game, my team had the ball and the girls passed it around. I concentrated on who had the ball and where it was being thrown. It was passed to me, and I caught it. I dribbled, looking for an opening so I could shoot a basket. Girls crowded around me. I couldn't move to an open spot. I looked for one of my teammates who was open, and I passed the ball to her. She passed it to someone else, and that person made the shot. ☯

Concentrating on the ball, openings and which teammate was clear, helped Addison reach her goal of playing well as a team member.

Focus to Reach your Goals

Brittany Basile

Brittany is a junior Black Belt and in the third grade.

I learned to concentrate at tournaments where I compete in forms, board breaking and sparring.

Sometimes I would get nervous and make a mistake when I competed with two others at the same time in the same ring. I have learned not to look at anyone else when I'm doing my form. If I look, I might make a mistake and have to fix it. I've attended about four or five tournaments now. It gets easier each time to concentrate.

At school, I do my work and ignore the people around me who are talking. At home, I concentrate on doing my homework when my 2 1/2 year old sister is running around and playing. ☯

Brittany did better at school when she took the concentration skills she learned in the tournament ring and applied them to doing her schoolwork, whether she was at home or at school.

Emily Roeske

Emily is a 2 time National Forms and Sparring Champion in NASKA - the North American Sport Karate Association. She has appeared in the movies 3 Ninjas - High Noon at Mega Mountain, Little Rascals, *and* Halloweentown *and she has done commercials for Barbie, Honda, Mattell, McDonalds and Campbells.*

Like my brother, J.P., I started martial arts training at a very young age. And like my brother, I was in newspapers and magazines. I followed in his footsteps, winning national karate championships and then on to the auditions.

I want to give auditions my best shot. So I do push-ups or a few kicks to pump me up right before I go into an audition.

Because of my size, it is difficult to find stunt people to perform my stunts. So I do them. For a McDonald's Mulan commercial, I performed martial arts skills. Sometimes stunts involve running, climbing and balancing.

Karate has helped me focus and concentrate. These skills came in handy on the set of *Halloweentown*, a Disney original movie. I had lots of lines to memorize and lots of physical scenes, and we had just four weeks to complete the project. I was the youngest cast member and it was important that I stay focused and get the job done.

Being able to concentrate helped Emily learn her lines and do her part even as the youngest cast member. Stunt work requires excellent concentration so that no one gets hurt.

Jared Michael Fox

Jared is a Black Belt. He started studying karate when he was four years old after watching the fun his brother was having in class.

We take timed math tests in my class at school and have to do 50 problems in a short period of time. I like math and am good at it, but I practice it a lot.

I remember what I learned in karate class about concentration and taking one step at a time. I think about the test before I take it, practice the problems, and then look over the test when I get it back from the teacher. I usually do the problems before the time is up.

Jared prepares by breaking the large task into small steps which help him study and test well.

Dan Casey

Dan started studying karate a little over six years ago. A first degree Black Belt, Dan is working toward his second degree.

My mom wanted me to take karate because it would help me concentrate better. In second grade all of the classes were in one large room. I could hear my teacher, plus two others at the same time. It was hard for me for the first couple of days, but I used what I was learning in karate and concentrated hard—to listen only to my teacher.

Recently, I was accepted into the Midwest Talent Search program for middle schoolers. I get to take practice ACTs early and prepare for college right away. I want to be a police officer.

Dan has set goals for himself. He wants to go to college and become a police officer. In order for him to reach these goals, he had to succeed at earlier steps. Using the concentration skills he had learned in karate, he was able to focus on his teacher and his lessons.

Courtesy

    An Everyday Warrior's actions toward others are courteous and polite regardless of who the people are or how you really feel about them. An Everyday Warrior doesn't have to respect another person, before being courteous.

    Responding courteously allows you to control situations and, in a way, other people's reactions to you. This includes being polite to brothers and sisters, parents, teachers, neighbors and peers.

    Being courteous and polite allows the Everyday Warrior to live in harmony with others and to get along with them. There might be rough moments but the situations won't get any worse because of something the warrior says or does that is impolite.

    Often drivers swear at other drivers and become very angry. This affects their ability to drive safely. An Everyday Warrior doesn't allow the anger of others to fuel his or her anger, but responds courteously and often lightens the situation and helps others see how silly their actions are.

Matthew George

Matthew is a 12 year old, red belt studying free-style united arts.

Our school holds two gym classes at the same time, but at opposite ends of the gymnasium. Afterwards, we line up in the hall before being dismissed.

After class one day, a boy from the other class came up to me and pushed me. He wanted to start a fight. He called me names and made fun of my family.

A couple of my friends egged me on to fight him. (Not many people in the school like this boy because he is always making fun of people.)

"Come on, Matt," they said. "You can do it."

I ignored my friends.

"You know," I said to the boy, "you're going to get into trouble if you try to get something going." And I walked away and got into line. I chose a spot near the front of the line. I didn't want to rat on him, but I wanted to make it impossible for him to do anything else at that point.

Knowing the martial arts gave me the confidence I needed to walk away and not get into deep water.

Matt exhibited a self-confidence that has taken root inside him. He reacted calmly and courteously. He didn't have to fight in order to prove something. He knows the only person he has to answer to is himself, and he knows his strengths.

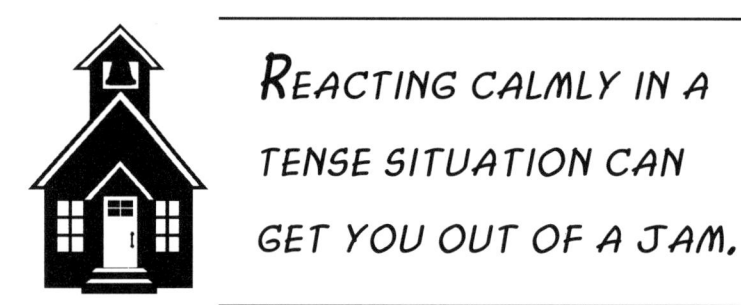

> REACTING CALMLY IN A TENSE SITUATION CAN GET YOU OUT OF A JAM.

Michael Patrick Castle

Michael is 10 years old and a yellow belt in kempo karate.

Our school was going to perform "The Wizard of Oz." I wanted a part, and I tried out for the role of Toto, Dorothy's dog. We were all sent notes which listed which people got roles.

The next day, a boy told me to come out to the back of school because he was mad. He wanted the role.

I just told him that maybe he could do better in the 8th grade play. "You could try harder," I said.

That made him angrier. I kept talking.

"Just keep trying," I said. "Maybe you will get a part next time."

He said "okay" and then he left.

Michael responded courteously and encouraged the boy to work hard and try again. By not acting defensive or getting angry because the boy was angry, Michael kept the boy focused on the issue—not on Michael.

Ken Martin

Ken is a brown belt in taekwondo.

At school, kids fool around and tend to tease each other. At the lunch table, one kid would always physically bully others. Before I became seriously devoted to martial arts, I thought this kid needed to be taught a lesson: that you don't always win situations through brute strength. I verbally crushed him, cut down after cut down. It seemed as though he was about to snap.

When lunch was over, he confronted me in the hall. He wanted to fight me, but I knew it wasn't right (especially in school). So I walked away, or tried to, but he relentlessly pushed me from behind. Once he saw I wasn't going to fight him, he left.

The main reason I didn't stand up for myself is because I didn't know how to fight. I knew if I did something, someone would have gotten seriously hurt because I didn't have any self-control. So I decided the best way to gain self-control was to go back to my martial arts school.

I relearned the taekwondo oath and tenets as well as a poem written by my instructor, "Just One Word." Through this simple poem, I learned that what I did was wrong since words can hurt just as badly as hitting someone.

So I try to watch what I say now, and I try to treat others as I would like to be treated.

Ken learned that words can be just as violent as actions and that courtesy can make a difference.

Riley Churchill

Riley is training to compete for the ATA World Champion title in the age 8 and under division, Black Belt.

I learned in martial arts to never give up. I learned to never quit in any sport, to always try my best and that it is good to compete—win or lose.

I used to get angry easily when things didn't happen the way I wanted them to. Now I've learned to have more patience with other people and myself. When I play baseball in the park, sometimes I get struck out. I don't like it, but I don't quit. I try to do better the next time.

It's the same in class. When I don't do a kick right, and I mess up and fall down, I do it again.

I also learned how to be polite and courteous and how to keep my patience with others. Now that I'm a Black Belt, I help out other ranks with their forms, one-steps and sparring. I get to hold the clapper pads so the other students can kick them and sometimes I get to stand up in front of the whole class with the other helpers.

I help out a couple times a week with the younger children in the Tiny Tiger class. When they punch with the wrong hand or kick with the wrong foot, I get a little mad but I don't show it. I keep teaching and just say, "Please switch your foot." The kids are only three to six years old.

Riley has discovered that reacting with patience is a form of courtesy, and he stays in control of the situation. Also, because of his reactions, he is allowed more responsibility.

Bill Peck

Mr. Peck is a Taekwondo instructor.

I'm on active duty with the United States Navy. Every day I deal with customers who are unhappy with the way we are doing things. My job is to keep the customers away from all the people doing the work.

During the war with Iraq, a customer entered the weapons shop. He was angry because his equipment wasn't ready. He yelled at me, swore, and called me names.

Instead of letting the incident drive me over the edge and yelling back at him, I took a deep breath and talked. I calmly explained to him that we were having trouble taking care of everybody's orders because we were getting ships ready to go overseas. I told him we were short-handed and working on lots of equipment.

After a few minutes, the customer calmed down.

Since I've been taking the martial arts, I find that I don't give up as easily as I used to. I have more control over my temper and reactions. I deal with problems myself and don't pass them along to others to handle. ☯

Mr. Peck responded courteously to what the man wanted, not to his inappropriate comments, and so was able to calmly handle the situation.

Oriana Hunter

Oriana is a Black Belt. When she was 10 years old and teaching taekwondo to nursery school children, Oriana was featured in a television segment highlighting outstanding children.

During social studies, the teacher suddenly noticed the new name-brand shoes one of the boys was wearing and began making fun of them.

"I know those shoes. Those shoes are gay."

The boy was really embarrassed and didn't know what to say.

"Mr. Blank," I said. "If you mean 'gay' as in happy that's one thing. But if you're using it the way most people use it today, that's inappropriate."

At that point, many of the other students joined in.

He apologized several times during the rest of that class. ☯

Oriana confronted the teacher's actions but in such a courteous manner that he couldn't get mad at her for the way in which she handled it. He had to take responsibility for his actions.

慈悲

Empathy

Everyday Warriors have empathy. They can imagine how others might feel even though the Everyday Warrior might never have had their experiences.

Empathy leads to compassion. Compassion is the result of knowing what another person is feeling, taking action and making changes. Everyday Warriors do something about the suffering around them.

Actions of an Everyday Warrior are based on what they learn by seeing events through others' eyes. This ability requires courage, because what you see might not require other people to change but require action or change within yourself.

Sometimes, empathy can enable you to destroy an enemy by turning him or her into a friend. Everyday Warriors focus on the good points of their enemy, things they admire and respect. Often this causes everyday warriors to change their opinion and turn someone they dislike a lot to someone they like. In the process, they have destroyed an enemy.

Jason David Frank

Mr. Frank played the role of Tommy, the White Power Ranger, for five seasons on television and in the two Power Ranger movies. He has acted in several independent films and has developed pilots for possible television series. Mr. Frank teaches at his own martial arts school and has three children.

☯ I've always been a dreamer. People used to listen to me talk, then look at me and say things like, "Jason, you're such a dreamer."

It didn't bother me. For me, my dreams were realistic goals. I wanted to be an actor and a successful business person. I wasn't going to give up my dreams just because someone else didn't think I was being practical.

I'm 25 years old, and I really understand now the importance of following dreams, whatever they are. I have found that to succeed, one needs discipline and dedication.

It's like running a marathon. Some run all the way to the finish line, while others quit before they get there. I set my goals and relied on my discipline and dedication to achieve them.

Fulfilling dreams as well as keeping them alive takes planning and work. To me, success is jumping out of the bed (even at 4 in the morning) and feeling excited about what the day is going to bring. I believe that whatever profession people choose, they should feel excited about it.

The Power Rangers have 30 to 40 million viewers. Last year, I traveled around the world, talking with kids and sharing what I know about martial arts. Visiting with them gave me the opportunity to let them know I am a real human being, not a super being.

However, I do think I have the super powers of dedication and discipline which help me juggle my roles: dad, business person, role model and martial artist.

Being a Power Ranger has allowed me to help others, to do things that to me are important. The Make A Wish Foundation told me about a girl whose dying wish was to meet me. I flew to Texas and spent a couple of days with her. It was only a few days out of my life, but it meant everything to her.

This is only one child whom I made happy. I don't give up just because I can't do everything for everyone at once, but I can affect the lives of individuals and make a difference one by one. ☯

As a role model, Mr. Frank takes his responsibilities seriously. He does what he can for the young people he comes into contact with and lives his life as an example to others.

Tony Atkinson

Tony, a second degree Black Belt, works harder on his own skills when he is teaching others.

☯ I like teaching other kids karate. If they are not doing a technique properly and just don't seem to know how to fix it, I help them correct it. And when they do it successfully, I give them a high five. They feel good because they've accomplished something, and I feel good because I helped them.

A few months ago, one student had a hard time learning his form and didn't do it very well in class. After class, I worked one-on-one with him. We went through the form, step by step, again and again. It was fun working with him.

Finally, I asked the instructor and his parents to watch us do the form. I stopped in mid-form and the student continued and showed them that he had learned his form. Everyone was really excited. ☯

Tony's empathy and care for the other student and his growth in karate resulted in the other student learning his form and feeling proud of his accomplishment.

Tina Claypool

Tina is a Black Belt.

☯ After being in taekwondo for awhile, I began to feel proud of my successes.

On my way to the tournaments, I noticed the homeless, including children, doing whatever they could to raise enough money for a hot dog. I realized that in order to be really proud, I needed to do something for others, not just for myself.

I began looking for projects. I collected un-needed materials from families for the Salvation Army. My friends and I helped out a few times at a soup kitchen for the homeless.

For two years, I volunteered at the nursing home where my mother worked. I usually helped serve breakfast and lunch and visited the patients, keeping them amused and entertained.

I became a counselor for my peers and met with them after the school day ended. I was able to help and encourage them as well as find solutions to my own problems through these discussions.

Every year, I participate in our taekwondo school's kickathon to raise money for children with Muscular Dystrophy. I love to help others. And in the process, I've discovered my own strengths. ☯

Tina's compassion takes the form of action. She becomes involved and does what she can to ease the suffering of those around her.

Josh Basile

Josh is a Black Belt in taekwondo.

☯ One time I was with my friends playing baseball at my old school's playground. A ten year old came up, and he had a cigarette. I told him he shouldn't smoke, and he said some older kids forced him into it.

I'd heard of those people, so I could picture them. He said he was going to go to the gas station and steal something.

I asked, "Did they force you to do that, too?"

I told him to stay and play baseball so he wouldn't steal. He played with us for an hour and went home.

A couple of days later I saw one of the kids that the ten year old said had forced him to smoke. I asked him why he had done that, and I told him that he better not do that anymore because the boy was only ten years old.

I saw the boy the next day. I told him he should try to stop because I just had a talk with the 15 year old who'd forced him. A month passed, and I saw him on his bike. He wasn't smoking anymore. ☯

People respect Everyday Warriors. Everyday Warriors share their strength with others.

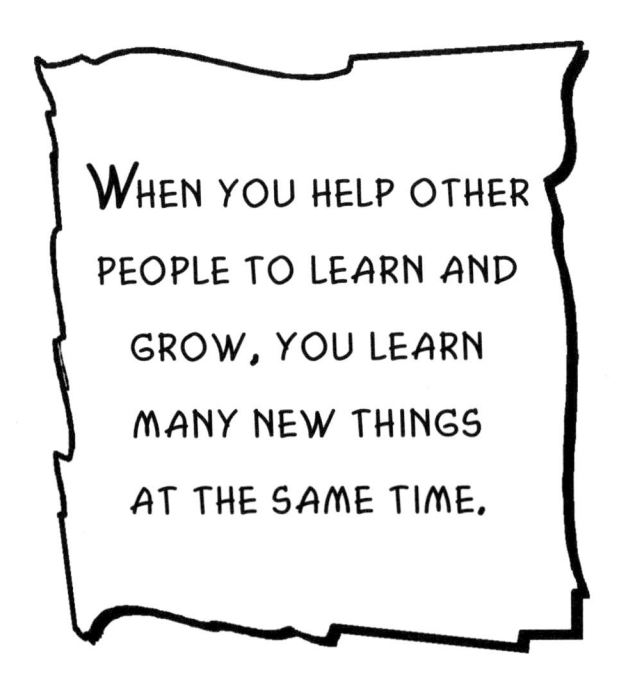

> WHEN YOU HELP OTHER PEOPLE TO LEARN AND GROW, YOU LEARN MANY NEW THINGS AT THE SAME TIME.

Perseverance

To persevere, Everyday Warriors set their goals and work hard to succeed. They might become temporarily discouraged by difficulties which slow their progress, but they continue in spite of them.

Difficulties can range from outside events happening to a person over which he or she has no control, to personal limitations which have to be worked around. To succeed, the Everyday Warrior keeps to the task, breaking down the large goal into smaller goals. Doubts might arise, but they don't stop progress toward the goal.

Everyday Warriors are self-motivated and dedicated. They are totally committed to reaching their goals and don't give up. They are disciplined and take the time to train and work at becoming the best they can. Goals may be different, but the way to reach them is through discipline. Everyday Warriors work each day at improving themselves, so they can become the best at whatever it is they want to be or do.

Cynthia Rothrock

Ms. Rothrock is a martial arts film star with black belts in five martial arts styles. She was ranked the number one female kata (forms) champion in 1982 by Karate Illustrated *magazine.*

☯ Martial arts has molded my life. I started at the age of 13. I watched my girlfriend's parents practice karate, and thought this would be a unique sport to learn. Not to mention the fact that to wear a Black Belt was quite appealing to me.

Class was not like I expected. It was extremely hard. It didn't help matters much that I was the only girl in the class. I felt uncoordinated. I couldn't shout and my punching was awful. I was on the verge of quitting when the instructor gave a speech to the class. His words were, "If you aren't any good, it's your own fault because you don't practice."

After my instructor's talk, I thought if I put my mind to it and practice harder, maybe I would get better. So I started practicing more and my punches became powerful. I felt more coordinated, and it got to the point where I was very confident in what I was doing. I found I was a natural and developed rather quickly. I loved it. But I had to get over the initial negative attitude of "This is too hard, I can't do this."

I won my first championship when I was an orange belt. At that time women's divisions were not divided into classes so I had to compete against black belts. To my surprise, I won!

I entered tournaments every week, collecting over 200 trophies. On the advice of other professional competitors, I started the professional circuit. From 1981 to 1985, I won first place in every competition I entered.

The same year I retired from competition, I had an offer to star in a movie in Hong Kong. My new career became doing movies. I moved to Los Angeles and signed up for acting lessons. My martial arts training taught me to always strive to be better and better, so I found out who the best acting coach was and made an appointment with him. I was nervous and excited.

As I began to read my monologue, he stopped me and screamed, "Why are you screeching at me?" Now I became full of panic, and he continued to yell. "You're not good enough for my group class. You must take private lessons." The cost was about $200 an hour. To make matters worse, he said, "How did you get the part anyway?"

I cried all the way home, which was now about a four hour drive since I had hit the famous Los Angeles traffic. Again I was ready to quit. But because of my martial arts training, I decided I wouldn't give up. I thought, "I'll just find another acting teacher I'm comfortable with and work at the process of acting to get good, just like I did with the martial arts." So I found another teacher.

Instead of allowing myself to focus on being upset and worried, I said that for whatever reason this has happened it's for my own good, and something better would develop. I turned my disappointment into a positive belief that things would get better.

Fortunately, I starred in another movie four months later and have been working ever since.

Through my martial arts training, I've learned to never accept failure, to be positive, and to always strive for my goals and work as hard as I can to accomplish them. ☯

Ms. Rothrock trained hard to perfect her skills and become a champion. In spite of her accomplishments, she ran into an acting coach who treated her with no respect. Rather than accepting that person's view of her, she remembered who she was and found another coach. She persevered, becoming the foremost female martial arts movie star.

Gina Matos

Gina is a Black Belt in hapkido.

☯ When I was in the seventh grade, I was a member of the Beginning Chorus at Southwest Junior High School in Palm Bay, Florida.

Tryouts for The Ensemble were coming up!! Each of the students have to sing a song in front of the class. Right away, I started to get really nervous and very afraid to sing in front of the class.

We had two days to pick out a song. I picked *He Ain't Heavy, He's My Brother*, one of the songs we sang in class.

I was getting so scared. I started to shake a little bit, because I knew that it would be my turn tomorrow.

Later that night, I went to my taekwondo class and the Grand Master was explaining about one of the tenets of taekwondo. Self-control! Self-control means to be able to be in control of yourself. We did exercises during our meditation portion of the class using inhalation and exhalation breathing techniques. It was as if he was talking to me and knew what I was going through in my head.

Well that night, I was thinking. "Maybe I can do this myself. I can go in front of that class and sing my heart out. All of my friends and family say I sing very well, so maybe I can give it a try."

My mom always told me to believe in myself and that I can do anything if I put my heart and mind into it.

The next morning was the first day of the tryouts. I wasn't the first one up, but I inhaled and exhaled slowly. I kept thinking of the night before. "This is nothing to be scared of. There is always a second try," I thought.

It was my turn. The fast beating of my heart started to slow. I was going to be okay.

I sang the song. Everyone liked it. I made the cut to be in the Ensemble, but I had to wait until the spaces were empty. I was put into the Ladies Ensemble in ninth grade. I had such a wonderful time. That just goes to show you that you can do anything if you put your heart into it. As long as you try and believe in yourself, you can accomplish your dreams. ☯

Gina had to face her own fears about how good she was before she could face the auditions. Using the breathing skills she'd learned in martial arts classes, she gained control over her fears and succeeded.

SOMETIMES PERSEVERANCE MEANS FACING YOUR FEARS, EVEN WHEN YOU DON'T THINK YOU CAN.

Justin Margotto

Justin, 17 years old, has studied karate for over 11 years. He was ranked number one in the nation in forms for three years and for one year in weapons.

☯ A year ago when I was 16, I tore my ACL while doing my form, "Perseverance," at the Diamond Nationals. I was just about finished. I jumped in the air, did a scissors kick and the wrong leg landed first. My knee went numb, and it popped. My whole knee felt like it just shattered.

When I fell down, I saw everybody looking at me. I felt kind of embarrassed because you usually don't see anyone fall and hurt themselves while they're doing forms.

People ran up to me and asked if I was all right. I didn't know what was wrong. They helped me up, and I limped out of the ring. My knee was swollen.

I couldn't compete in the rest of the tournament. Back at the hotel that night, my knee swelled up even more.

The next day when I returned home and went to the doctor, he did a few tests and told me I had torn my ACL. I asked him what my options were. He said I could leave it alone and have a slight chance of ever competing again, or I could have surgery which would allow me to compete as much as I wanted. I knew the choice I had to make - surgery.

My parents were scared for me. We sat down to talk about the options and whether I actually wanted to go through with the surgery. I did.

But the day of the surgery, I was scared. I kept thinking, "What have I gotten myself into? I can't believe this is happening to me. Would I ever be able to do karate again the way I used to?"

The day after surgery, I had my first physical therapy session. To me that was the hardest part of the whole process. They tried bending my knee. It hurt so badly that I cried. But they said it was going to help, so I let them do what they had to do.

I dreaded going to therapy. I knew there was going to be pain whenever they worked on my knee. But I had to do it to get myself back to where I was before.

I went to therapy three days a week for three months before being given instructions to do my own therapy at home, twice each day. My parents and friends reminded me that I was going to be doing karate again in no time.

As soon as I could, I entered tournaments. I still had a screw in my knee. I won eight first places and four Grand Championships. I wasn't completely back, but at least I was doing something I loved.

But I still had pain in my knee even though my ACL had healed. This time, the doctor told me I had torn the meniscus in my knee, and that I needed more surgery to repair it and remove the screw. I had competed in five tournaments with a torn meniscus as well as the screw in my knee.

After the meniscus was repaired, I entered a competition, this time in the adult division, and I won first place. ☯

Justin had already become a national champion and had performed as part of a team. He was blocked from advancing further by the injury. But hard work and perseverance have enabled him to return successfully to the tournament circuits and continue practicing and teaching.

Juan Moreno

Mr. Moreno won two Silver Medals at two Olympic Games. He is a motivational speaker and is managed by Champion Management.

☯ Growing up, my younger brother Carlos and I did a lot of sports. One day during the off-season of hockey, Carlos and I happened to stop for lunch at a local hot-dog shop. Right next door there just happened to be a martial arts school. So after lunch, we all walked next door to have a look in the window.

Someone was there. My Dad knocked on the window and the man came over to let us in. It turned out that my Dad actually knew the man inside. They were friends from the past. He was the assistant instructor at the school. After speaking with him for awhile, my father was very impressed with the program and asked if we would like to give it a try. We both said "yes" and came back that very night to sign-up and start classes. I was almost nine years old.

After I had practiced for a month, my instructor announced a tournament that was coming up and asked me if I would like to have a go at it. Everyone told me that I was good, so I expected to go and do really well.

I lost that first tournament in about 30 seconds. Losing was horrible for me. All I could think about was that now I would have to tell all my friends that I had lost.

I walked out of the ring, head down, kicking the floor, and sniffling because I was crying.

My father said, "Hey, what are you crying for?"

"Well, because I lost."

"If you can walk out of that ring, son, and look me in the eye and say, 'I tried my best, trained hard, didn't give up and listened to the coach,' you have nothing to be ashamed of. But if you walk out of that ring and realize that you didn't do all of those things, you should be ashamed because you didn't let me down or your coach down or anyone else down. You let yourself down."

It was hard, but that little talk always encouraged me to push myself to the next level. I don't worry about letting people down, because I know if I don't give my best effort, I will let myself down. And then I will always ask myself, "what if?"

Two months later the USA Junior Olympics were coming up. This time, I was determined to practice even harder and win a gold medal. I did, and it was a big deal for me. When they hung that gold medal around my neck, I felt the difference between winning and losing.

Until my dad was there to greet me with that familiar question, "How did you do?". I was confused at first, then he said, "Remember what I asked you before. That is what matters. What type of effort did you give? Son, there are going to be days that you win and days that you lose. But if you give 100 percent, you will always be a winner."

From that day on, I never lost a Junior Olympics match again.

If I am able to make it to the 2000 Olympic Games, it would make me the only taekwondo athlete in history to be in three Olympic Games. And there could be the possibility to actually medal; that would put me on the same level as some of the most famous athletes in the world. Three Games and three medals sounds pretty good.

I won the Silver Medal in both the 1988 and 1992 Olympics. In 1988, I was only 17 years old and not expected to make the team, let alone earn a medal. It was the first time I had ever traveled outside of the USA to compete. I was supposed to be very nervous and inexperienced. I had to use all of my past to mentally deal with that intense level. I was able to convince myself that I was the best that my country had to offer, and that was all the confidence I needed. I fought hard and came home with a Silver Medal.

In 1992, the situation was the exact opposite of 1988. Four years later, I was the veteran of the team and one of the favorites for the Gold Medal. I had won virtually every tournament at the national and was in the top two internationally. I felt good, but I didn't have the day that I needed. I lost to a better fighter on that day. I earned my second Silver Medal. At another time, who knows?

I am often asked how I was able to excel and achieve at such a young age. I tell them that my formula for success has always been my three D's. Every successful person in life has to have these three qualities to make them a total winner. They are: Discipline, Dedication, and Desire.

Personally, I had a lot of success as a youngster. It would have been easy for me to become full of myself and think I had all the answers. I had to have the Discipline to take advice and criticism in order for me to continue to learn and advance.

It was also necessary to have the Dedication to commit and sacrifice myself in order to achieve the things that I set as goals. It is easy to become distracted with work or play, but it takes that special person that is willing to persevere through all of life's obstacles.

I had all of the peer pressure of growing up in an urban area. All of the temptations of hanging with the wrong guys or simply following the wrong crowd were staring me in the face on a daily basis. I cleared all of those negatives away so that I could stay on the path leading to my goals.

Lastly, my favorite part. Desire. Having the feeling deep in your heart that makes you have discipline and dedication. That feeling can be felt when no one else is around. When you are all alone, and you say, 'One more mile, one more kick.'

The special thing about this word is that no one can give you it. People can want you to be successful, to be happy or whatever . . . but desire has to come from you personally. I had that Desire in me. I wanted to be different and accept the challenges that were in front of me.

All of this leads me back to what my father said at my first competition. I still live by that motto today. Every morning when I look into the mirror, I simply ask myself, "Am I being the very best person I can be?" "Am I working toward my goals?" This is my personal reminder to keep me on the track of a Champion for Life. ☯

Mr. Moreno perseveres. Ever since he was eight years old, he has set goals. His father taught him that he could win mentally, physically or in both ways. Following this guideline, Mr. Moreno will always be a winner.

Jenny Nice

Ms. Nice owns and teaches in her own studio. She has won six American Taekwondo Association (ATA) World Champion titles since 1989. She is the ATA Regional Chief of Instruction and Regional Representative and is a member of their World Demonstration Team.

☯ My mom was involved in the martial arts two years before I joined. I was in high school and had other interests. I was active in all kinds of competitive sports, was track captain and worked part-time.

When my mother got her Black Belt, I said, "That's it, if my mom can be a Black Belt then I can too." I started in my senior year of high school. I was 17 years old, and I thought that I'd seen and learned a lot during the years that I had watched my mom. I found out that it was a totally different story actually participating in taekwondo.

I hadn't realized how competitive taekwondo could be. I fell in love with it and the tournaments. After two weeks of lessons, I competed in my first tournament and won two first place trophies.

My goals changed. Before taekwondo I had planned to go to college and become an accountant. Now, I wanted to do and study taekwondo all of the time.

So after graduation, I continued studying taekwondo, continued my part-time job and also started another part-time job teaching aerobics at the taekwondo center so that I could be there more often.

After I had trained for two years, my instructor left the organization and I trained with another instructor. I traveled many miles to continue my training.

I finally decided to open my own school. From that time forward, teaching and owning my own studio were my goals.

I started teaching in 1988. One of the things I had to learn was that it was okay to be a woman and run a taekwondo business. In the beginning, people told me I needed a man to help run the business. I had a partner who assisted me part-time, while he worked a full-time job. I ran the taekwondo business full-time as the business could not afford to have two full-time employees. After a while, I found other successful schools run by female instructors, and I decided that I was going to go for it also.

In 1990, I bought out my business partner. I went from making shared decisions to realizing this was now my own business, and I could make my own decisions. And I did. The school became a success. At one time, I was operating two schools, one in Michigan and one in Indiana. It was a hectic schedule, but I was doing what I loved for a living.

I set my goals high. I want to keep learning and inspire others to reach their own successes. I even convinced my ex-partner to open a taekwondo school in the town my mom lives in and now my mom is a certified instructor and a two time World Champion. ☯

Ms. Nice had concerns about her ability to run a taekwondo school just because she was a woman. As she gained more experience and confidence, she persevered and no longer let that fact hold her back. Now, she helps others succeed and attain their dreams.

Kaely Mc Dougall

Kaely is an 8 year old purple belt. She began studying karate when she was five years old.

When I first started karate, I was shy. In karate, I learned that my mind is the strongest muscle in my body and how to control it. I learned how to believe in myself.

After taking karate for a year, I decided to take a break to try other challenges like soccer, piano and ice-skating. I scored goals in soccer, gave piano recitals and competed in ice-skating.

After awhile, I remembered that a very important code to the martial arts—dedication, which means to "never give up"— was one of the main reasons for my success in all of these challenges. So I started back in karate after a two-year break, and I just received my purple belt.

I was put into the TAG (Talented and Gifted) program at school. It is hard, especially math. We have to do math facts — 100 problems in five minutes every other week. After we pass one test, we go on to the next area. The first test covers addition, the second test covers subtraction, third is multiplication and the fourth is division. The final test covers all four areas.

We take these tests every other week. They let us know how we did. My dad types up on the computer the problems I need to work on, and I practice them at home. I practice and practice. I'm on division right now. As soon as I pass all four, I'll go to the fourth grade level. I'm not going to give up.

I now realize that one of my many goals in life is to be a Black Belt and help build a better community.

Committing herself to do well in all of her activities, Kaely practices and works hard to succeed. She perseveres.

Arthur (AJ) Rafael

AJ, age 10, is a recommended Black Belt. He started studying taekwondo when he was five years old.

I failed to get my Black Belt on my first try. I had promised my Mom that I would, and I didn't. I didn't feel good about it, but I continued to think positively. I practice at home a lot. I'm training hard so I can get my Black Belt the next time I test.

I do many things along with studying taekwondo. I play basketball with my friends, and I play piano and clarinet.

I began practicing the piano over five years ago. I started the clarinet last year. I practice so much that my parents hired a private clarinet teacher for me.

I have lots of things to do. I want to do well in all of them. I focus on each thing I'm doing while I'm doing it. I don't want to think about a piano recital when I'm working out in taekwondo class.

AJ did pass his Black Belt test. He didn't allow his earlier disappointment to stop him from reaching his goal. His determination not give up and ability to focus on what he is doing, have led to success in several areas.

Devin Hurley

Devin, four years old, is studying kempo karate.

I practice the kicking and punching a lot. When I wake up in the morning, I practice. Once, I woke up in the middle of the night and practiced my kicks and punches at 2 a.m. After I practiced awhile, I went back to bed.

Devin is persevering. She wants to do well and practices every chance she finds, even at 2 in the morning!

Herb Perez

Mr. Perez won the Gold Medal at the 1992 Olympic Games in Barcelona, Spain; three Gold Medals at Pan American games; and a World Cup Championship. For six years he served as captain of the United States National Team. Mr. Perez is the Director of Market Development for Century Martial Arts Supply.

☯ Right after winning the World Cup Championship in 1987, I lost the Olympic Team trials. This was totally unexpected.

I had trained for the U.S. Olympic team for two years. I had won the team trial eliminations, then I lost in the finals to someone I had beaten four times before.

I had to decide whether to retire and get my law degree or to put my life on hold for another four years and continue training and competing so that I could try again in 1992.

This was a difficult decision. It costs a lot of money to train for the Olympics. And I had no money; I was living day to day.

But, ever since I had started competing, I was determined to be a member of the U.S. Olympic Taekwondo Team. I couldn't quit now. I chose to try out for the Olympic Team again in 1992. I would refine my training, and I would make the U.S. team.

At the 1988 Pan American games, my opponent kneed me and I tore my medial collateral ligament in my left knee.

Now I had to decide again if I would retire or if I would undergo surgery and the months of painful rehabilitation. If I retired, I could finally get my law degree. I could spend time with my family. But I wouldn't have made the Olympic Team.

So I put my plans on hold while I trained, traveled and competed around the world. I wanted to be fully prepared for the 1992 Olympic Team trials. Things were different this time. I won the 1992 team trials and could finally represent my country on the United States Olympic Taekwondo Team. I competed in Barcelona and came home with a Gold Medal.

I was lucky. I had refused to surrender. I stayed until I actually won. My debts were paid off and I promised myself that I would help other athletes finance their training. ☯

Mr. Perez refused to retire before he was ready. He knew by experience that money is a problem for athletes training for the Olympics. Mr. Perez decided to do something about it. He and Gary Hestilow, President, as well as David Wahl, Vice President, of Century Martial Arts Supply have established an Athletes for Excellence Fund to provide support for the top athletes. Mr. Perez' determination to fulfill his goal helped him win. It is his continued perseverance that is making it easier for other athletes to fulfill their dreams.

Kevin K. Marshall Jr.

Kevin is an orange belt, studying Kempo Karate.

Our class worked on a science experiment that used a B+B solution. My partner and I did one experiment that showed that B+B reacts to a breath of air and to water by dissolving. The water returns to a clear color. Then we mixed the same solution (B+B) with vinegar and water and used an air pump. We watched the B+B dissolve into small particles and turn the water bluish-green in color. I explained the experiment to the class. I used to be shy. Now I like to talk, perform in plays, teach and make people laugh.

Through perseverance Kevin is growing into a well-rounded Everyday Warrior.

Quinn Sweeney

Quinn studies kempo karate.

☯ "I have a friend who used to call me "Finn." I don't like that name. It's not mine. Every time he would call me "Finn," I would say k k k - Quinn. When he started calling me "Feeney," I would say Swe, Swe, Sweeney. I taught him how to say Sweeney, and he got a pencil."

Quinn's story told by Mrs. Sweeney:
The K (Q) and S sounds were hard sounds for Quinn's friend to say because of a speech impediment.

His friend was often over at our house, and I always heard them talking.

"You can do it," Quinn would say, "Okay, buddy. K, K, Quinn. Say it real slow."

It took a long time, about one-and-a-half years. The boys were in pre-school together as well as kindergarten. Quinn often translated for his friend.

Once, when my husband picked the boys up from school, his friend said. "Hey, Mr. Feeney. You have any tookie at home?"

My husband thought for a second. "Yeah, I think we have turkey."

"Dad, it's not turkey. He wants a cookie. Do we have any cookies at home?" Quinn said.

On field trips, they sat together on the buses and Quinn would repeat the routine.

"K. K. Quinn. Swe. Swe. Sweeney."

In kindergarten, Quinn always responded to his friend the same way.

Last November, all of a sudden Quinn's friend yelled, "K. Quinn Sweeney."

Everybody gave him high fives and cheered. The kindergarten teacher sent him to get a special pencil from the office. She wrote a note home to his mother who called to thank Quinn for helping her son. ☯

Quinn had a goal in mind. He wanted his friend to call him by the right name. So he constantly corrected his friend and had him practice the sounds. By persevering, by believing this could happen, Quinn helped his friend overcome a speech impediment.

ACHIEVING YOUR GOALS THROUGH PERSEVERANCE CAN TAKE A LONG TIME, SO DON'T GIVE UP!

調和

Harmony/Balance

Everyday Warriors are in harmony with others and themselves when they keep all of their feelings and actions in balance. Their emotions are stable. One emotion, such as anger, doesn't control their actions and feelings.

Everyday Warriors are centered. The person they are dealing with may not be in balance. When people react in anger or for personal gain, these are signs they will ultimately fail. Doing something out of love or enjoyment can lead to success.

Benny "The Jet" loves to fight and has won many kickboxing tournaments. When he is hit, he doesn't respond in anger because the other person ticked him off and made him mad. He acknowledges the good hit and looks for an opening. He is a strategic fighter and a winner. He is calm and comfortable in the ring.

The same holds true for Bill "Superfoot" Wallace. He never loses his temper in the ring, because "then I'd make a stupid mistake."

In daily life, when Everyday Warriors lose their tempers, they are no longer balanced. They have lost their calm center and can do things they might regret later. Conflicts result if people are out of balance. When people get along with each other, they are in balance and harmony.

Christopher Matos

Christopher is a third degree Black Belt in taekwondo. He and his mother co-authored a book about Attention Deficit Disorder, Pants With Pockets and other tips on Managing an ADD/ADHD Child.

I am not a tall kid, but it seems all of my friends are taller than me. When I was in the fifth grade, they used to call me names like "inches" and "shrimp." It made me feel very sad and mad to think that my friends would keep calling me something that bothers me. I told them to stop, but they kept it up.

I told my instructor about it when I went to class. He told me that kids would tease him when he was young and he used to feel just like me.

"The best thing to do," he said, "is to not let them know it bothers you. If you can't ignore them, try to think to yourself that they are only kidding. Don't take it upon yourself to handle the situation."

He also said that getting angry is not good and it uses my energy in a bad way. I should not let others control my feelings.

I try really hard to remember what he told me. I have tried to laugh it off and say things like: "Let me put that in writing." But at times, I tell them that I don't feel good and walk away from them. If they get me too upset, I can always talk with adults I trust.

Christopher is developing his self-esteem so he won't give others control over his actions. He is working hard to keep his center and his feelings and actions in balance.

Jesse Goldberg

Jesse, a Black Belt, studies kenpo karate. Now in tenth grade, he started when he was eight years old. In 1996, Jesse was named Youth Underbelt Outstanding Weapons Competitor of the Year with kamas. He especially enjoys the strategy involved in sparring.

I learned you don't do something and end up being surprised by the outcome. I ask myself questions such as "Is it right?", "Is it wrong?", or "It's risky and if I get caught, can I deal with the consequences?"

At the end of a basketball game last year we had just beaten the other team by one to two points in a last minute comeback. They were upset.

After the game, we lined up to shake hands with the opposite team. One kid shoved me. I knew I could beat him up, and I wanted to do it. But I thought, it's not worth it because I'd probably get into trouble and be suspended. So I said to myself, "No, it was just a little thing, let it go."

Jesse has learned that taking control of his behavior and thinking of the results of actions, has put him in control of his life.

Amethyst Anderson (Amy)

Amy is a Black Belt in karate.

I was afraid to try new things because I might not be able to do them. But every time I did something I didn't think I could do, my karate teacher pointed out that I had done it.

I like to sing. I was very nervous the first time I performed in front of a crowd, but I liked it. Now I act and sing in a lot of school plays. For our Christmas show, I sang a solo, "A Time for Peace."

Once Amy accepted that she had accomplished things in karate, she was able to expand and participate in other activities such as singing and playing the violin. Her confidence to try new things is part of her balanced life.

Sara Urquidez

Ms. Urquidez has been in the martial arts for 24 years and has taught for over 15 of those years. She is married to Benny "The Jet" and helps run their school.

☯ Many of the students who come to my kickboxing class think they're learning kicking and punching, but on another level they're learning how to deal with their emotions and fears.

At the beginning of each kickboxing class, we do a breathing technique workout which I call "Centering Time." It centers their energies. When their energies are balanced, it prevents them from getting hurt and prevents the fears and emotions that keep them from growing.

I believe in the power of energy. If I show fear, it empowers others. If I become angry, it feeds their anger.

Late one Christmas night, I was shopping. I was walking in an underground parking lot, my arms full of Christmas packages, trying to find my car. I couldn't remember where I had parked it.

I sensed someone walking behind me. "Oh now what," I thought, but I didn't let on right away that I knew he was there. I just stayed focused on his location.

I told myself just to concentrate and be aware, not to feel fear. But I did feel fear and have butterflies. So I did the breathing techniques and centered my fear and emotions.

I remember turning around, dropping my packages and going into a self-defense stance. I stared at him. I didn't say anything. It bothered him.

"Hey, can't you hear me?" he yelled. I just kept looking at him. I had to keep my focus right on his eyes because if he took his eyes off me, or if I looked away, he could regain his confidence. I know he felt something from me - my centered energy. I never said anything, just stared. Finally he said, "You're a crazy chick!" and he ran off. ☯

Ms. Urquidez centered her emotions. By staying calm, she didn't give him anything to build off of. He couldn't get angry because she wasn't angry. She was in control of the situation because her emotions were balanced.

Ashley Farrow Schmidt

Ashley, a junior Black Belt, started studying taekwondo when she was six. In 1998, after winning the Wisconsin championship in forms and sparring, Ashley went to Orlando, Florida and competed in the Taekwondo Junior Olympics.

I have found that faith has helped me a lot. In taekwondo, school and everyday, it helps me focus on what I am doing. Faith gives me the courage I need at times when I am scared. At the Junior Olympics it was just after lunch, and I was getting ready to spar. I weighed in one pound too heavy for my usual weight class, and I had to fight girls who were bigger than anyone I had ever fought before. I prayed. I believe without it, I would not have done as well. I lost, but my Dad said I fought the best fight of my life. I got hurt a little, but I didn't quit. Without faith, I probably would have quit. ☯

Ashley uses her belief to help calm and focus herself so she can do the best she can.

David Repetny

Mr. Repetny has a fifth degree in kenpo karate and a third degree in koshyo-ryu kempo. He has also studied tai chi and taekwondo.

At first, I thought karate was all about fighting. Now I know its about coexisting with other people. Blending and coexisting with others is a daily business with me.

I teach in an African-American high school. When I first started, it was difficult. Where I had grown up, I didn't have many opportunities to learn and understand another person's culture.

After I spent some time in the school and observed the other teachers, I realized I needed to blend in order to be effective. So I researched African-American history and got to know my students.

I've learned through my study of the martial arts that a relationship exists among all things. The base of all life is harmony. When we focus on similarities instead of differences, we blend, coexist and succeed. ☯

Discovering how to live in harmony with those he teaches and works with, enables Mr. Repetny to accomplish his job and help others succeed.

Bernie Fritz

Mr. Fritz, a seventh degree Black Belt, is the national supervisor of Independent Karate Schools of America (IKSA) which also has schools in Europe and Canada. He teaches tai chi and stress management classes to other schools and large companies, and delivers seminars around the world.

I attended a party right after I got my Black Belt. I sat with two people whom I know pretty well, and we started talking about the martial arts. These two had never studied the martial arts, and they wanted me to show them what I could do. I wouldn't.

That made them angry and they started questioning my abilities. "How good are you really?" they asked.

I didn't want to brag or even be in this discussion.

"I don't care how good you are. I don't think you can take both of us," one of them said.

For a moment, my ego was insulted. I was angry. I was almost ready to take up the challenge and show them how good I was.

Then I remembered that I don't have to accept what people said about me. I had learned to refer to my spirit, not my ego. My spirit is who I am. Whatever they said certainly wasn't going to take it away from me.

So I smiled and agreed with them. "That might be true. But I promise you one thing - one of you will go to the hospital."

Suddenly everything changed and turned to laughter.

It made me feel good because I deflected the anger and turned it into laughter. ☯

Mr. Fritz didn't let his anger control his actions. He remembered who he was and that they had no control over him. He responded confidently and calmly and eased a touchy situation.

名譽
Honor

    Honor is a personal code that includes honesty, fairness to all, keeping promises and a willingness to accept responsibility for one's actions.

    Honor is accepting the consequences of something that happened because of what a person did or didn't do. Consequences aren't always bad. They can also be good. A person with honor accepts responsibility so that projects can be finished.

    Honor is lived out in all of your actions and is based on what you consider to be morally and ethically right. A person's honor is quite obvious to others.

Bernd Stab II

Bernd is in the pre-med honor program at Old Dominican University.

☯ One of the most important people in my life is my grandmother. She had a choking accident the summer of my senior year. Her brain suffered some damage because she couldn't breathe for ten minutes. As a result, she can't walk or talk as well as she once did.

I know the frustration and disappointment I felt when I couldn't do things I once could do. I know what it is like to suffer pain that is so bad that a movement as simple as placing one foot in front of the other is impossible.

In high school right after my first degree Black Belt test, the doctors found that I had growing problems. A bone that usually grows in the heel wasn't fusing (connecting) properly and couldn't protect the joint. Every time I kicked or jumped on the hard surface, I jolted the joint and kept it from healing. I stopped training for a year, and I used the time to learn how to teach taekwondo to children.

A year later the pain left. I started training again for my second degree. While my heels were no longer much of a problem, my hip was. When I did certain motions, my hip would pop out of place and then I couldn't lift my leg.

I was 16 when I tested for my second degree. My hip popped near the end of the test, and I wasn't able to finish. I had done well up to that point, and they allowed me to finish the test on video tape. However after a week of rest, I still couldn't do it. I was very disappointed, but that's the way it had worked out. I had to deal with my disappointment and go on.

When my grandmother suffered brain damage, I knew I wanted to help take care of her. I couldn't do this if I went away to college so I stayed home and attended the university in my city.

I visit her on weekends and try to get her to think and play games. We speak German, because she doesn't know much English. She can't walk by herself now, so she holds onto my arm, and I walk her around the house. I would like to get her to a point where she can walk on her own.

I don't know how long she's going to be around. I'm there for her because it's important to me that she knows there is someone who cares for her and always will. ☯

Bernd follows a personal code of honor which he demonstrates by his actions. He keeps his promises to his teammates, to his grandmother, and to himself regardless of what it might cost him in time or pain.

SOMETIMES KEEPING A PROMISE MEANS GIVING UP SOMETHING YOU WOULD RATHER BE DOING.

Michael Johnson

Michael is a high brown belt in taekwondo.

I was playing with my friends on the school grounds one weekend. At the time, I was a second level brown belt. Kids in my school who knew I was in the martial arts came up to me and asked me to beat up another student - just for kicks.

I told them "It's against the rules. 'Never misuse taekwondo.'" And I walked away.

Michael showed honor by accepting responsibility for his actions. He believed beating up another student was wrong and refused to do so. The others might make fun of him but he knew he was right and acted accordingly.

HAVING HONOR MEANS BEING RESPONSIBLE FOR YOUR ACTIONS.

Matthew Chiera

Matthew is studying kempo karate.

One of my best friends and I are always whispering in French class when we're supposed to do our work. We know it makes our teacher angry when we do this, especially while she's trying to talk.

One time, the teacher thought my friend was talking and called him up to the desk.

"I want you to take a note home to your parents, and I'm going to send you to the office," the teacher said.

I spoke up. "It was my fault. I was talking to him. He wasn't the one making the commotion at all."

"It's your fault then?"

"Yes."

"Then please don't do it again," she said.

When I stood up and told the truth, I turned something that would be bad for my friend into something better.

In speaking the truth, Matthew demonstrated a personal code of honor. Matthew couldn't let his friend take the blame and the consequences for something Matthew had done.

Michael Windham

Michael, 10 years old, is a Black Belt in karate.

My dad was in his 60s when I was born. He started forgetting things when I was five, about the time I started taking karate lessons.

Four years later, my Dad was officially diagnosed with Alzheimer's disease. I was really busy with my karate, violin, Cub Scouts, school and piano, but I wanted to help my mom take care of Dad so he could stay home.

It was hard. He couldn't get as involved in my activities as I would have liked him to do. Sometimes he would try to help us without realizing that he was creating more problems for us. He would do things like open and throw away mail. We couldn't have our mail come to our house anymore and rented a post office box.

When my friends came over, I would have to tell Dad that they were my friends and not strangers so he wouldn't worry.

I loved and respected my father. He was a big responsibility, and I wanted him to be around as much as possible. He might have been forgetful, but he was kind to me. He died a few months ago when a cancer he had ten years earlier returned. ☯

Michael loved and honored his father and even though he was young he helped out as much as he could so his father could remain at home.

Jae Kyu Lee

Grand Master Jae kyu Lee began studying taekwondo in Korea when he was 10 years old. Later, he opened his own taekwondo school and taught the police in Seoul's Police Department. He also studied a 2000-year old healing art called acupressure. He moved to the United States in 1975, and taught in a friend's school before opening his own.

My school's focus is the family. When I teach classes, I'm concerned with developing the whole person. My three-part philosophy consists of developing strong health, teaching self-defense, and enabling young kids to become good champions in life. I believe the best investment in our future is to teach and change a person's life.

I get all of my students involved in caring for one another and in helping each person to be his or her best. Six years ago, one of my students had leukemia. He's ten years old now and doing well. But his family needed help paying the large medical bills. I wanted to do something which would help, so I organized a school board breaking fund raiser to raise money for him.

Now, one of our major projects each year is a fund-raiser to support cancer research at the Milwaukee Children's Hospital. Each student, whether adult or child, is given five boards. They raise money for each board, whatever amount they can get. Then, in a huge event held at the school, the students break the boards. They raised $15,000 in 1997 and over $20,000 in 1998. The Milwaukee Children's Hospital awarded us a plaque for our contributions. ☯

A man of honor, Grand Master Lee's actions and teachings reflect his beliefs.

人本

Humanism

Everyday Warriors show humanity when they treat all others with respect, kindness, and fairness. The power of Everyday Warriors is shown by their concern for others.

They support others with actions and words and work to improve things. Everyday Warriors go out of their way to do service projects in their community, school, church, synagogue or temple. Their actions are based on wisdom, knowledge, and empathy.

Benny "The Jet" Urquidez

Benny "The Jet" Urquidez, one of the superstars of kickboxing, retired from the ring with a 57-0 record. He medaled in five weight divisions. Mr Urquidez has written several books on the martial arts and done many training videos. He appears in movies and gives seminars around the world.

☯ I love teaching, and I believe I'm a better teacher than fighter. Yet fighting is what got me here to this point in my life.

When I was three years old, I put on boxing gloves. My mother was a professional wrestler, and my father was a professional boxer. All of the boxers trained their children, and we competed against each other. I competed in the boxing ring when I was five. It was a sort of pee-wee boxing.

Judo became popular in the late 1950s and early 1960s, and I took judo when I was six years old. I began karate lessons at age seven. Then in 1973, I discovered full-contact karate. I opened up the Asian kickboxing circuit to American fighters. In a way, I became an American ambassador. They invited me to fight in their countries and showed me their best fighting techniques. I was able to see at firsthand things no one else had yet seen.

Since I couldn't fight in tournaments forever, I started making movies and giving seminars all over the world: Japan, South America, Europe, Australia, Africa.

I found that people are people—the world over. They have the same hunger, same needs, same wants. All are looking for the same thing - peace of mind.

To me, peace of mind is the power to love from within. That's when I decided that whatever I give I will give it as a gift. After I give something, it can be used however the person wants to use it. They can even give it away. I don't believe it's a gift if I attach rules on how to use it.

I like to give something every day of my life. Sometimes the gift comes in an unusual form.

After class one evening, one of my students kept telling me that another student was stealing my t-shirt.

"Sensei, that guy is stealing your t-shirt," he said.

"No, I gave it to him as a gift."

"But I just saw him put it into his bag," the student said again. "He stole it."

"No, I gave it to him."

I know I can always replace the t-shirt. He is the one who has to live with himself. I went home that night and slept well, at peace with my gift.

To me that is true love, giving something to another without any ties or expectations of receiving something in return. ☯

Benny "The Jet" believes in treating others with kindness and makes sure his daily actions demonstrate his beliefs.

Mark Andrew Rogian (Drew)

Drew, a red belt in karate, especially likes sparring.

In school one day, some girls chased one of my little friends and took his book bag. I told them to give it back, and eventually they did. I felt it would be a lot better for things to be worked out than for someone to have a bloody nose. ☯

Drew stood up for one of his friends, and did it in such a way that everyone benefited and no one was hurt.

Sam Johnson

Sam is studying kempo karate.

When one of my friends in pre-school was doing a really tough thing at school he needed someone to help him. No one wanted to do it. He was trying to count to 1,000 by 10's and write it on a sheet of paper. He didn't know how to write 100 or 1,000. I was doing something else, but I decided to put it away and help him. ☯

Sam is a beginning martial arts student. As he studies more, he will reinforce the value of helping others which he learned from his parents.

Gerald Fisher

Gerald is a purple belt.

My confidence has improved since I've been in the martial arts. Before, I rarely raised my hand to volunteer to help others in class. Now I speak up more, and I'm more willing to help others with their projects.

In art class, we made book jackets out of paper bags. We cut the bags open, glued pictures to them, wrote descriptions of the main characters in our book and what their feelings were, and described the story on the back cover. I finished early and when other kids needed help gluing, coloring, and folding the paper jacket to cover the book, I helped them. ☯

Gerald showed his concern for others in the class by helping them complete their tasks.

HELPING A FRIEND IN NEED IS AN IMPORTANT PART OF BEING AN EVERYDAY WARRIOR.

Kathy Long

One of the leading female martial artists in the world, Ms. Long retired from professional kickboxing in 1992. She holds five world champion kickboxing titles. She was the stunt double for Catwoman Michelle Pfeiffer in Batman Returns. *Ms. Long is a member of the Black Belt Hall of Fame.*

☯ I was 15 when I started martial arts. I had a friend in high school studying Aikido, and she invited me to watch a class. I fell in love with it the moment I saw it. I felt Aikido provided me with a more spiritual outlook and gave me time to understand my body and what I could do with it.

I've continued in the martial arts ever since, studying a variety of styles including Kung Fu San Soo, Kali, Wing Chung, Brazilian Jiu Jitsu, boxing and kickboxing.

I don't like conflict. I come from a childhood of conflict so I avoid it if at all possible. The martial arts enabled me to take care of myself in many different situations. It also made me less tolerant of other things. I stick my foot into situations many people would ignore.

Driving home one sunny afternoon, I passed a man walking his dog on a leash. The man was angry. For some reason, he screamed at the dog, smacked and kicked him.

I screeched the car to a halt, jumped out, grabbed the leash from the man's hand and stepped back about ten feet.

The dog cowered behind me. He wouldn't respond to the man when he called him. It was as if the dog knew where it was safe.

The man yelled at me, "You have no right to interfere."

The dog was pretty small, a Border Collie mix. About the only thing it could do was bark. It was completely at the mercy of this man.

"No. I can't let you have the dog."

"It's none of your business," he yelled. "Get away from me. Leave me alone and give me my dog."

"I'm not going to let you abuse the dog anymore," I said and let him know exactly how I felt about his treatment of the little dog.

Finally, the man gave up and stormed off. "All right. Take the dog," he said.

It was nice the man left. I found the dog a good home. He was such a sweet dog. Of course it was none of my business, but I saved a dog's life. ☯

Ms. Long doesn't like conflict but she will not ignore injustice. She goes out of her way to help those (animals as well as people) who can't help themselves. Through her involvement, she makes others stronger and puts them in positions where they are able to take care of themselves.

謙

Humility

    Everyday Warriors don't brag about their successes. They live and act modestly, recognizing the importance and contributions of those around them.

    Everyday Warriors don't believe they know everything there is to know about the martial arts or about anything in particular. They realize they can learn from anyone, regardless of age or gender. This makes them well-rounded and more successful.

    Everyday Warriors help others and treat everyone as an important person. The successes of Everyday Warriors don't make them greater than any other person. They are humble in their attitudes toward others.

    Everyday Warriors know themselves and their capabilities. They maintain a deep self-confidence and inner knowledge of who they are. They don't feel the need to prove anything to anyone else or care what others judge them to be. With this inner knowledge, self-esteem and self-confidence, they don't have to brag or not be themselves to gain acceptance from other people. The only people Everyday Warriors have to prove anything to are themselves.

Larry Lam

Mr. Lam did the martial arts for Leonardo in Teenage Mutant Ninja Turtles II: The Secret of the Ooze *and* Teenage Mutant Ninja Turtles III. *He portrayed the evil character, Warlock, on the TV series* WMAC Masters.

I lived with my grandparents in Hong Kong and started studying martial arts when I was four years old. I both loved and hated it. It was not fun. I studied three to four hours a day.

Soon after, I moved to Canada to live with my real parents. But until I was 14, I moved around a lot between different foster homes, group homes and family friends. I went to 12 elementary schools.

In Vancouver, when I was ten years old, I studied taekwondo. I took class with twenty other people, all adults. I didn't like the martial arts until I saw my heroes George Chung and Cynthia Rothrock in a demonstration. Then I got excited again. I couldn't afford lessons, so I practiced every night at home.

I entered my first competition, May 10, 1980. I had no clue what I was doing. But I won the tournament and brought home a six-foot trophy. It was great.

Mom said, "You paid $20 for that?" After that, I never asked them to watch me compete or told them when I was going. That was the only time I showed them my excitement towards the martial arts and winning. Dad used to use the trophy as a coat rack.

courtesy of Claim 2 Fame Photography

When I was 15, I decided to move from Canada to California so I could train and compete. I spent six to seven months saving the money I got from teaching martial arts to adults so I could purchase a plane ticket. Then I told my parents I was leaving.

I found an instructor who offered me room and board if I taught and trained with him. I stayed with him until I graduated from high school. If I did have a father figure, it was my martial arts instructor.

I started competing in the NASKA circuit. Every year, I was rated top in my division in forms and in the top 10 in fighting. In 1990, I did some movie fight scenes with Jet Li, plus some low budget action films. From there I did two *Teenage Mutant Ninja Turtles* movies and *WMAC Masters* television series.

I learned one of my most valuable lessons when playing the role of Leonardo in *Teenage Mutant Ninja Turtles II*. I was 19 years old. People treated me very well—always hanging around, talking to me, and looking up to me. I took it for granted, became arrogant and expected this type of treatment all the time.

Then one day, with two weeks left of filming, a couple of us (Donatello, Michelangelo, and me) were pulled high up inside a net and a wire snapped. We fell to the ground when we weren't expecting it. I hurt my head and back; the others were hurt too. The film people just said, "Okay, bring in the other guys."

I was disposable. I was only important to them as long as I was on top. Once I fell and couldn't work for a short while, I was no longer of value to them. I realized they didn't really like me, but the position I was in. That realization has kept me humble. I learned from this to be a good role model for others.

I travel around the world, talking to people, giving speeches and seminars, acting in films, and teaching students. People come up to me and say things like, "We started martial arts because we saw you at a demo and you talked to the kids at school."

I couldn't be a good role model or share my love of the arts if I was a jerk or arrogant and didn't make martial arts exciting for kids. One of the best things I do is teach students how to be confident, to carry themselves in more positive ways and to have more control of their lives.

Mr. Lam's experiences growing up helped him develop his self-confidence and learn his own strengths. On the movie set, he learned to evaluate why some people liked him and realize what he was looking for in true friendships. Adjusting his behavior to reflect what he has learned about people, he has taken on the responsibility to help other youth develop their own positive inner strengths.

Howard Jackson

Mr. Jackson was the 1973 Black Belt Hall of Fame Fighter of the Year, the first Black American fighter to be ranked number-one in professional karate. He was the first karate champion to be ranked in professional boxing (number 6 in the world by the World Boxing Council). Currently, Mr. Jackson is the road manager and training partner for Chuck Norris.

I dropped out of high school three times. I started studying kung fu in Detroit in 1967 after the Detroit riots. When I was 14, I saw Chuck Norris' picture in a magazine. I knew then that I wanted to be good enough to be on the cover of a martial arts magazine.

A roomer staying at our house went to kung fu class, and I began taking classes with his teacher. I thought I was pretty good, but I was at the "dangerous ground" level and too young to realize it. I fought with a bully, and he taught me a lesson—I didn't know as much as I thought I did. So I searched for the martial art that would work best for me.

I saw a guy doing a demonstration at a recreation center, and I didn't like his manner. He looked good when he showed self-defense moves and one step sparring, but he made a big point of showing how he would beat the other guy up if he caught him with his girlfriend. I knew his attitude was wrong. I told him afterwards that martial arts weren't for attacking people but to be used as self-defense and that you're supposed to be humble and confident, not a show-off.

I met his sparring instructor, Harold Williams, who practiced tang soo do, a Korean style of martial art. I learned he had a lot he could teach me, and I decided to switch styles and instructors.

From Mr. Williams, I learned good character, self-esteem, discipline, and perseverance. The martial arts gave me focus and a method by which I could achieve realistic goals. I learned that step by step, one small goal at a time, I could accomplish what I wanted. I returned to high school, graduated and entered the Marine Corps.

I studied with Mr. Williams until I reached Black Belt. I tested for my Black Belt at the same time Chuck Norris tested for his fourth degree.

At my first tournament, I met Chuck Norris and Bob Wall who had watched me compete. After I was disqualified, they commented on my good kicks and asked if I had just gotten off the boat from Korea. They also told me I needed to work on control and learn more hand techniques, and that they were willing to teach me.

They invited me to work out with them, and Chuck said I could stay at his house. I caught a Greyhound bus from San Diego to Los Angeles, and Chuck picked me up. The next day, I learned better kicks and fighting techniques. After that, I worked out every weekend at Chuck's school.

Joe Lewis also played a part in my success. Joe was my sparring partner. He taught me Bruce Lee's theories and fighting strategies as well as his own fighting theories which had revolutionized professional karate. While Chuck, Mike Stone and others gave me the tools, Joe sharpened them.

That first year, I ranked number seven nationally. In my second year, I had risen to number one in all weight categories. I won several grand championships and national titles, and started appearing in magazines.

When I had a knee injury in 1974, I was devastated. Ralph Krause, Karyn Turner, Chuck Sereff, Al and Malia Dacascos held a "Help a Brother" tournament to raise money for my surgery. Their support taught me a lot about having friends in the martial arts, about the internal desire to overcome, to win, and to stick with something until it's completed.

Toward the end of my competing career, Chuck asked me to work for him as his road manager and his training partner. I worked for him for 10 years, then I left to broaden my experiences. I worked for five years as the road manager for the Temptations, before returning to work with Chuck.

I don't feel I accomplished what I did all by myself, but with my friends in the martial arts. It's building, growing, sharing, and giving something back to others. When roadblocks get in my way, I modify my course and keep trying to reach my goals until I attain them and find contentment within myself—no matter how long it takes.

Mr. Jackson learned early that he didn't know it all. As soon as he was open to the many people willing to teach and work with him, Mr. Jackson rose to the top. He ran into many setbacks including a severe knee injury, but with the help of others as well as a strong determination, he again succeeded.

不屈

Indomitable Spirit

Indomitable spirit is the determination to reach your goals. Everyday Warriors keep on doing something whether they feel like it or not at the time because their goals are important. They train even when they aren't pumped to do so, because they want to improve.

Indomitable spirit is courage. It takes courage to face fears of failure, to face imagined as well as real fears. Everyday warriors don't let these fears stop them or keep them from trying their best. They strive to overcome their fears.

Everyday Warriors have a sense of commitment to their goals, a plan which they follow. But the route to success they've mapped out is adaptable. It yields and finds ways to succeed just like the young tree that lives because it is flexible enough to bend in the wind, as opposed to the tree that can't adapt and bend but stands rigid, breaks and gives up when faced with difficulties.

It requires endurance to reach one's goals. The Everyday Warrior, while continuing in the general direction of attaining goals, is pliable. There is no need to be rigid and rely on only one method to reach success. The Everyday Warrior is confident he or she will reach the goal. This inner strength and calmness lets others know the warrior means business and is confident that the goals will be reached.

Sang H. Kim

Master Kim has written eight martial arts books and starred in over 40 instructional video tapes. He enjoys traveling around the world helping students and instructors improve their skills. He is also a highly skilled calligraphy artist, awarded the top prize in Korea, and all of the calligraphy you see in this book was written by Master Kim.

☯ After the Korean War, my country was completely ruined. My parents had to work for 18 hours each day to support 14 family members. After school, all of my family had to help my parents farm. My favorite time came when my older brothers would show off their martial arts skills in the field after their work was done. Sometimes they taught me and after a while I became good at performing with them.

When I turned 15, I left my house. I had to move to the city to go to high school. My parents couldn't afford for me to stay in the dormitory, but I wanted to go to a good school so badly that I found an abandoned gym and lived there by myself near the school.

The gym had been abandoned for a long time. It looked like no one lived there after the war. Bats and centipedes were my roommates and right next door was a cemetery.

Some of my friends at school told me there were ghosts. They told me people who got killed during the war lived there as ghosts, and they showed up on rainy nights in bloody white gowns. When they told me, it didn't bother me because I didn't believe them.

Then one night, it was quite stormy and rainy. The wind banged the door and woke me up. The lightening scared the bats from under the ceiling. The wings of the bats made shadows on the walls. I knew I didn't believe in ghosts, but I couldn't stop thinking about them. I began to feel weak. It scared me. The gym was in an isolated place, so there was no one I could run to for help.

Then I began to see the ghosts. They showed and quickly disappeared. I thought about when I was a little boy and how strong my brothers were when they practiced their martial arts. So I got up and stood in horse riding stance. I punched and punched. I yelled and yelled. "Kiya, Kiya, Kiya, Kiyaaaaaaaaaaaaaaaaa,.........."

It must have been thousands of punches and Kihaps.

When the storm stopped, I went out of the house carefully. There were no ghosts. The storm had blown the straw roof off of another house. That was the ghosts I saw during the night. The martial arts that I learned from my brothers saved me that night. Although there were no real ghosts that night, the ghost was in my mind. My kihaps and punches helped me to be strong.

When my father helped me get a room in the school dormitory a year later, I had to say farewell to my friends, the bats and centipedes. Two years later, I became a National Taekwondo Champion. My best coaches, to be honest with you, were the darkness, poverty, the storm, the ghosts, the bats and centipedes. They taught me how to be strong and to overcome fear so that I could face even the most difficult times in life. ☯

That night, Dr. Kim faced his fears and realized he had the strength to deal with whatever storms he might encounter.

Suzann Wancket

Winner of a variety of grand championships including the Battle of Atlanta, Blue-grass Nationals, Arnold Schwarzenegger Classic and the US Open, she also won two diamond rings at the Diamond Nationals. As an adult, Ms. Wancket twice won the AKA Warrior Cup. "Do not let anyone discourage your dreams," she said. "You have to follow your heart and remember you are your own destiny."

☯ I am dyslexic. I never liked to read, talk or perform in front of people. Now, because of the martial arts, it is what I do for a living.

These abilities didn't appear overnight. It took a long time for me to gain confidence enough in my martial arts skills to feel comfortable competing. I prepared and practiced for hours before each competition.

Through it all, I learned a process that I use to succeed in other areas of my life.

I grew up in a suburb outside of Chicago. I am a third degree Black Belt in shorei-ryu at John Sharkey's school. I gravitated toward the children who couldn't hang out in a fast-paced class, took them under my wing and taught them.

Since my career was in ophthalmology and doing research for eye diseases, I moved to Minnesota to work with Dr. Campbell, one of the top innovative ophthalmologists in the country.

I enjoyed my work. But one day, after returning from a vacation back home, I sat in Dr. Campbell's office and said, "I miss my students back home at the karate school."

Dr. Campbell told me I should meet Dr. Jeffrey Alexander, a pediatrician who specialized in ADD (Attention Deficit Disorder) and ADHD (Attention Deficit Hyperactive Disorder).

We met in June 1992. I told Dr. Alexander I wanted to teach karate and knew I would have a school some day.

"How about I refer 10 of my patients to you and why don't you teach them here in the Medical Center's workout room?" he asked.

I jumped at the chance.

But first, I returned home to test for my Black Belt. Afterwards, back in Minneapolis, I met again with Dr. Alexander.

He said, "You'll start teaching in February 1993."

"What about March?" I was nervous about starting right away.

"February."

"March."

"February."

"Why February?" I asked.

"I don't know," he said.

"March?"

"No. Feb. 3."

So I started in February. He sent me 10 children who had a variety of diagnoses such as hyperactivity, autism, depression, or ADD. Three weeks later, he watched me teach and commented on how much the children had improved. "Suzann," he said, "Don't ever give up on these kids. They need you, and society lets them go."

He left the room. I didn't even see him go. That weekend he attended a pediatric seminar, went to a scenic point, took pictures, fell off the cliff and died. I never had the chance to say good-bye.

I feel I was led to this spot in my life. When I had 40 students in my classes, I again talked with Dr. Campbell and told him I had to quit my research job and totally focus on the kids.

"I know," he said.

I now have 160 students who were referred to me by the doctors and a waiting list of another 100. I watch my students gain confidence, learn to focus, and succeed. Some are now taking acting lessons, who at one time were never sure they would be able to learn their forms. Others literally went from D's in school to B's. They tell me they know they can do well in school, because they are taking karate. Many enter school sports and some are even traveling around the country with me to compete in national competitions. ☯

Ms. Wancket's faith and indomitable spirit enabled her to plunge ahead in spite of her fears and to firmly believe in her life's work of teaching underprivileged children.

Megan Allen

(As told by Megan and her mother, Jeanne Langlois) Megan is a high brown belt in taekwondo.

☯ In March of 1995 when she was 13 years old, Megan had a full spinal fusion. Rods were placed in her spine from the base of her neck to her buttocks. Just a year earlier, she had screws placed in her broken ankle to help mend her growth plate which had been broken. Megan was confined to a wheelchair and not allowed to exercise.

When she was released from the doctor's care and given permission to exercise, Megan couldn't stand, bend, push or pull. She had many problems and had to continue to sit in a wheelchair because she didn't have the strength or ability to get out of it. All in all, Megan spent almost two years in a wheelchair.

I took her to a martial arts school and the master instructor worked with Megan on a one-to-one basis to help her gain balance and exercise her stagnant muscles.

After two years of taekwondo, she can now get off the mat to a standing position almost as fast as the other students. She breaks boards and has more confidence in herself. She has friends at the school; people who inquire about her when she isn't there.

She has lost weight and no longer needs a wheelchair, even for distances, because of the stamina she developed in taekwondo.

Mainstreamed into a keyboarding class in a regular high school, Megan's class work is improving. The master instructor has promised to take her to dinner when she attains all A's on her report card.

Watching Megan's growth and progress, experiencing the instructor's patience with her and their caring for her, has led me to also take martial arts classes. I see myself becoming more disciplined, coordinated and self-confident. Like Megan, I set my goals and each time I accomplish them, I feel an inner peace. ☯

Megan's indomitable spirit has helped her work hard. She set short-term goals she could accomplish and build upon toward her long-term goal. Step-by-step, Megan regained the strength to stand, to walk, and to bend. Her spirit and determination have encouraged her mother as well as others to keep striving for success.

Melissa Paone

Ms. Paone holds three World Titles in forms competition through the National Blackbelt League. She has been inducted into two Martial Arts Halls of Fame and has even had a Legislative Resolution passed in her name recognizing her accomplishments in the martial arts.

☯ I began training in the martial arts when I was 11 years old. It wasn't my idea to try karate lessons, but my mother insisted that it should help boost my confidence and give me something to do besides sit in my room and read all day. I decided it wouldn't hurt to try, and after my first lesson I enjoyed it so much that I began to train six days a week. At the time, I wasn't really concerned with improving my confidence. I trained because I was having fun.

The first time I noticed a change in my self-esteem was after I had been training in the martial arts for about a year. I was taking a Home Economics/Career course at school, and had to do a research project on "What I Want to Be When I Grow Up."

Who, at 12 years old, knows what they want to be when they grow up? I certainly didn't. Days and days went by with no ideas at all, until I finally decided that it would be interesting to interview my karate instructor and write my paper about becoming an instructor myself.

However, when I approached the teacher with my idea, she thought I was kidding and told me that I'd better get serious and get to work or I was going to fail the course. I told her that I was serious and that I had been training in tang soo do for about a year and liked it very much.

She said that she'd never heard of a female karate instructor and that I was just stalling because I couldn't think of a real job that I wanted to write my paper about.

I was stunned, because it was the first time I ever had a teacher openly discourage something that I really wanted to do. A year ago, I probably would have caved in and chosen a different topic for my project, but somehow, her resistance made me more determined to prove her wrong.

As it turned out, the research paper counted as half of our grade for the course, and I ended up passing by the skin of my teeth. This was mainly due to the fact that I had received such a low grade on my research paper which was declared "unrealistic" and "non career-oriented" by my teacher.

She insisted that she was trying to help me out because a karate instructor was a job that had no future. In today's world, where I could be anything I wanted, why would I choose a career like that? I guess she didn't see the irony in the situation.

Whenever I encounter anyone telling me that I can't do something, I think back to that Home Economics teacher, smile, and go ahead and do it anyway. ☯

Ms. Paone had an idea of what she wanted to do with her life. She didn't let others pressure her into not doing it, but she set her goals and worked to make her dream come true.

Steve Harrigan

Dr. Harrigan is a reporter/producer for CNN in Moscow, Russia and a 3rd degree black belt.

☯ The other day I was sitting behind my desk at work, afraid. Then I realized the feeling was familiar. I got my start as a reporter during the war in Chechnya, Russia. The reporter who was supposed to cover the story left after three days when Russian planes began dropping bombs. I stayed, and for the first time stood in front of a camera.

When I look back now at the tapes I see fear in my eyes and hear it in my voice. In a war of carpet bombing (bombs constantly shelling an area), guerilla attacks, hostage taking and atrocities, I was afraid of the camera.

It takes one kind of confidence to go into a war zone, the confidence that you can take care of yourself in a difficult situation. It takes another kind of confidence to talk in front of a camera, to act in front of an unknown viewer. When I began reporting I had one but not the other.

And when I felt fear the other day I realized I had felt it before . . .many years ago, before fighting in a tournament. A fear of facing an unknown opponent. I could feel it in my palms, in my breathing. Then I smiled at the comparison. I didn't have to fight anybody now, just stand in front of a camera and talk.

So maybe you are like me. Maybe you are afraid to fight and face up to your fears. If so, my recommendation is: Fight, face your fear. Whether you stand up to your fear with panic or confidence, it is going to happen anyway. There will likely be many more things through the years that you are afraid of. And none of them will be able to stop you. ☯

Mr. Harrigan's indomitable spirit helps him face his fears so he can complete the job he was hired to do and confront new challenges as they arise.

Lisa Conde

Lisa Conde began studying martial arts in ninth grade. As she continued to train, she set goals for herself. Her B's and C's became straight A's. Lisa is a junior in college studying for a business degree..

☯ Since the ninth grade, I had wanted to be in the Miss Denbigh pageant. However, I was too afraid to sing or dance, and I had no idea what I could do as my talent. I was also terrified of performing and speaking to a room full of people. After two years of taekwondo and competitions, I finally got the guts to try out in 11th grade for the pageant. I wrote Martial Arts Ballet as my talent on the application.

After they accepted me into the pageant, the coordinator asked me to put a little more ballet and a little less martial arts into the form so it would fit better in the show. I held my ground and reminded her the judges had let me into this pageant after seeing my routine.

"If they accepted it the way it is, I am doing it the way it is," I said. I could tell she was not happy, but I did my form and the audience loved it. That was a pivotal moment in my life. Although I didn't win the title, I felt like a winner that night and to this day because I conquered my fear and did the very best I could. That was one of the proudest moments in my life. ☯

Lisa's indomitable spirit gave her the courage to tryout for the title of Miss Denbigh and to do it in a manner with which she was comfortable. She didn't allow others to influence her to change her form just because it was different.

Danielle Stluka

Danielle is a Black Belt, studying karate

The school is holding a learning fair. My classroom teacher wants me to give a karate demonstration.

I am working extra hard to do my very best. I wish that I had more talent, but my karate instructor always tells us to do our best, not anyone else's best. So that's what I will do—my best.

Determined to give an excellent demonstration, Danielle is practicing and is confident she will do her best.

Luke Boucher

Luke is a second level brown belt. He studies shotokan karate and jiu-jitsu.

I compete in state and local tournaments in fighting, katas, musical katas and weapons kata. One time in a local competition I was performing my musical kata, and I totally messed up. I was so nervous, I forgot it all.

I made up a lot of moves to get back into the form. I impressed the judges because I kept on going. They could tell I made a little mistake, but not that I'd forgotten the entire rest of my form.

Luke discovered the success which comes from an indomitable spirit. Accepting the fact that he had forgotten his form, he didn't let that stop him. He quickly adapted and made up a new form. This allowed him to reach his goal of competing in that tournament.

HAVING AN INDOMITABLE SPIRIT MEANS NOT QUITTING WHEN THINGS GET DIFFICULT.

Bill "Superfoot" Wallace

Bill "Superfoot" Wallace won the U.S. Championships and the USKA Grand Nationals three times each. As a professional fighter, Mr. Wallace won 21 consecutive fights and earned the title of Professional Karate Association Middleweight World Champion. Black Belt magazine *twice named him "Competitor of the Year," and in 1978, he was elected Black Belt Hall of Fame "Man of the Year." He co-starred with Chuck Norris in* A Force of One *and appeared in 14 other movies.*

Bill Wallace and Bernie Fritz

☯ I had fun fighting in tournaments. However, I was afraid too. When you watch the tapes, you can see me lifting my face upward. I always said, "I'll take all the help I can," before I entered the ring.

There is never anybody in the ring who is not frightened. We never know when a well-placed kick will do serious injury. I've learned to use that fear to motivate me to do my best, to know that my opponent is watching every move I make, and to plan my moves accordingly so that I come out the winner.

I faced this fear outside of the ring a couple of times in my career.

I started out as a high school wrestler. When I joined the Air Force, I found they only offered judo, no wrestling. In the workout room, I wrestled with the judo master. I took him down a couple of times, and he said, "Good. Now put on this white jacket and let's try it again." He threw me all over the place, and I joined the judo team. That year, 1963, we made the Second Air Force Team championships.

In 1966, while training for the California State Championships, I worked out with an individual who was 210 pounds. I weighed 145 pounds. I came in for body drop judo throw (seiotoshi). He countered. I stepped between his legs with an inner reap throw (o/chigari). All 210 pounds of him collapsed right on top of my straightened right leg and destroyed my knee.

At that time, they didn't have the state-of-the-art techniques they use today for knee surgery. On me, they performed what they called "exploratory surgery." And they really explored. I was in a cast from my hip to my ankle for almost three months.

When a friend suggested we check out a nearby karate school, I hobbled there on my crutches. The instructors, Mick Gneck and George Torbett, told us we could train that day if we wanted.

I removed my shoes, stood at the back of the class and started kicking with my leg in a cast. They told me to always kick with my left foot while I wore the cast on my right leg. When others did 500 kicks on each leg, I did all 1,000 on one leg. When the doctors removed my cast, I continued to work out with one leg. I didn't want to kick with my right leg in case I hurt it some more.

After leaving the Air Force, I enrolled in college, studied karate with Glenn Keeney, and won my first tournament, the Mid-East Nationals in Lexington, Kentucky. When I turned professional, I never lost a kickboxing match. I fought from 1974 to 1981.

The fear returned full-force last year when I was faced with the need to have a total hip replacement. I realized my career could be over, and I might not be able to throw a kick ever again after this surgery. I might not be able to continue to give my seminars. But it had to be done, so I did it.

I have a master's degree in kinesiology, so I developed my own rehabilitation program. I walked the day of the surgery. The second day, I walked and climbed stairs. The third day I walked, climbed stairs and got in and out of a car. I went home on the fourth day and rode the bike. I stopped using the crutch eight days later. And I can still do the splits. Within 1 1/2 months after surgery I was doing my seminars and demonstrating my kicks.

I faced my fears, planned my moves accordingly, and things worked out pretty good. ☯

Mr. Wallace's indomitable spirit helped him adapt to his injuries. When he could no longer use both legs, he practiced on one and became the superstar known as "Superfoot." When he feared losing all of his mobility because of the hip replacement, he developed a rehab program which helped him reach his goal of still being able to do the splits so he could continue doing what he enjoyed - giving seminars and kickboxing demonstrations.

June Louise Elliott

June Louise studies taekwondo.

☯ Throughout my teen years I had one major goal. I wanted to become a FBI agent. In my sophomore year of college, I was diagnosed with Type I, or juvenile, diabetes. My dream seemed unreachable.

I had to give up so much, only to gain heartache: checking blood glucose levels, calibrating insulin with the amount of carbohydrates I ate, and no more parties. I felt robbed of my young adult years.

Shortly after my diagnosis, I received an issue of *Countdown*, the magazine of the Juvenile Diabetes Foundation. It featured athletes with Type I diabetes. One of the athletes profiled was a 29 year old lawyer who practiced taekwondo, karate, Thai boxing, and Jeet Kune Do.

I thought this type of training would distract me from my troubles and provide aerobic exercise on days when I wasn't weight training. I also thought it might enhance my chances of getting into a career in law enforcement. It was a win-win situation.

I started with karate, but my progress was slow; the instructor held classes only twice a week during the dinner hour. This caused me to have swings in my blood glucose (sugar) levels, and I couldn't give my full attention to class. I moved to a martial arts school with more classes that I could schedule around my college classes and track practices.

I feel complete when I train in weight lifting and martial arts. I feel like a victor, not a victim of diabetes. I compete well with other students despite the diabetes. When I find myself overwhelmed by my up and down blood glucose levels or become discouraged, I think about how hard a form was to learn, and how I finally mastered it. Kicking and yelling "kiai" releases a lot of tension and are very calming.

I train as an athlete with diabetes, not as a diabetic athlete. Although I cannot get rid of diabetes, I can oppose it with my indomitable spirit, giving it my best effort. I can achieve the most I can until a cure is found—giving my dreams a chance. ☯

June Louise faces her disease with courage and has the determination to continue to strive for her goals.

Arlene Limas

Ms. Limas was ranked nationally by Karate Kung-Fu Illustrated *magazine and was the national champion in creative forms at USTU Nationals before becoming a member of the United States Olympic team and winning an Olympic Gold Medal in 1988.*

☯ I started when I was five years old. My parents had signed up all four of my older brothers. While two went on to become black belts, two soon lost interest and went into other sports. My dad and I took over the two open memberships.

From the time I was seven until I was 25, I had never taken more than three weeks off in martial arts. I went four days a week until I grew older and could take public transportation. Then I went to class more often. I was there when the school opened, and I left when it closed.

At age 21, I had won nearly every event and had been ranked #1 for several years. I used to compete in all three events: weapons, forms, fighting. I was competing 65 times a year, sometimes two tournaments a day. I would go to one in the morning and to another in the afternoon if it wasn't too far away.

Competing in the Olympics in Korea was an awesome experience, almost story like.

The U.S. Team was the first team to move into the Olympic Village. One day, they rounded us up and asked if we would help prepare the technicians for the medal ceremonies in the arena. We did a test. When they lined us up, I was positioned in the Gold Medal spot. It felt so right.

Working out in the arena was amazing. Not everyone in the United States does taekwondo or is interested in it. But in Korea, we knew this huge, empty arena would be full of viewers. The taekwondo events were already sold-out.

I was scheduled to fight on the first day, the same day as the opening ceremonies. My coach wouldn't let me participate in them. I was upset. In my mind, going to the Olympics was a package deal. Many people compete and never leave with a medal. When I missed the opening ceremonies, I was afraid I had missed my whole Olympic experience. But it was warm, and the athletes marched all day. I would have been tired. The coach was right.

I fought Virgin Islands, Spain and Korea in the finals. My toughest fight was actually the second round that I fought against Spain. She was the defending world champ.

Though it is always difficult to fight Koreans in Korea and in front of their outstandingly enthusiastic crowd, I won the Gold Medal fight. I stood again on the Gold Medal pedestal, and they draped the Gold Medal around my neck. The flags were completely up and due to technical difficulties the United States National Anthem wasn't playing.

A huge contingency of the spectators were U.S. military forces. So when the United States flag was raised, and no music played, we just started singing. The music swelled from within us. We were almost finished when they were able to play our music. We started singing it all over again.

It was awesome. I didn't mind standing up there in the Gold Medal spot a little longer. ☯

Ms. Limas competed because she loved it. She set her goals higher and higher as she succeeded: local, regional national and then the United States Olympic Taekwondo team. She was upset when she couldn't march in the Opening Parade, but she didn't let that stop her. When the United States flag was quietly raised in her honor, she enjoyed the moment very much and didn't worry or complain about the lack of music. She and the others from the United States sang the National Anthem without the music.

Ernie Reyes, Sr.

Ernie Reyes, Sr., was inducted into the Black Belt Hall of Fame as Instructor of the Year. In 1998, he was identified as "The Master of Creative Karate" on national television and honored as one of the Greatest Martial Arts Masters in the 20th Century in a television special produced by Wesley Snipes.

☯ I am 53 years old now, and how time flies. When I was a young boy, I had a deep love for competitive sports. Ever since grade school, I had an intense, burning desire to excel in football, basketball and track. Through hard work, I achieved "best in the league" awards.

My passion for athletics continued into college. I set a goal for myself to work extremely hard and hope that I would receive a basketball scholarship. So while I attended junior college, I practiced all the time, waking up at 6 a.m. to shoot baskets even if it was raining. Many nights after I did my homework, I would stay up until midnight shooting more baskets under the lights of the stars.

To increase my strength, I also lifted weights at a local gym in Salinas, California. During these training sessions, I watched in amazement as a karate class worked out. Watching them became part of my routine. These Black Belts eventually became my friends and although I never worked out in karate, I told my first instructor, Moises Arizmendi, that one day after my basketball career was finished, I would definitely love to learn martial arts. Well, it happened sooner than I expected. I badly sprained my ankle, and my dream of a basketball scholarship died. Little did I know that it was a blessing in disguise. My purpose in life (for the rest of my life) was now created for me—martial arts.

I decided to take martial arts lessons, channeling all of my competitive energies into this new arena. My first intention was just to compete. I wanted to fight and win the big trophies. (But that goal would change to teaching.)

I advanced very quickly through the different color belts because of the many hours I had spent just watching classes.

I transferred to San Jose State University and taught every night for Grand Master Dan Choi who had just come from Korea (and is still my instructor). I stayed at the school for a least three hours each night. He taught me the essence of taekwondo: discipline and respect. He made me aware of the highest values of martial arts: honor, loyalty, family, bravery and to never use martial arts in a negative way but only for self-defense.

During this time I had to overcome many challenges. To survive, we were on welfare and used food stamps. Rain or shine, I rode my ten speed bike, 10 miles to work and back. During these hard times, I was soon given one of the greatest gifts of my life. Ernie Jr. was born.

I eventually graduated from San Jose State University. This was one of my biggest victories in life, since I had had a difficult time learning how to read in grade school. I had flunked kindergarten twice and first grade once. To make up your mind to never quit and to strive to improve yourself daily is very powerful.

I had promised my parents that I would graduate because they had always supported me during my hard times. I wanted to give back to them something that would show my appreciation

Ernie Reyes, Jr and Ernie Reyes, Sr.

for their hard work when they used to get up at 3 a.m. and do back breaking labor in the lettuce fields of Salinas.

The indomitable spirit in martial arts to never quit was instilled in me by my martial arts instructor and my parents. They were role models of hard work, discipline and love. ☯

Mr. Reyes' parents were excellent role models of indomitable spirit. Following their example, he achieved his goals in spite of injuries, hard times, and major setbacks. As a teacher, he shines as an example to his students.

Katelyn Sleznikow

(As told by her parents Dale and Rhonda and her brother David) Katelyn, 8, won the 1998 Perseverance and the 1999 Indomitable Spirit Awards at her taekwondo school.

☯ When Katelyn was three years old, we found out she had cancer in the upper thigh bone (femur) behind her left knee. If this had occurred in 1990 or earlier, her leg would have been amputated. Thankfully in 1995, the doctors had developed a new treatment program which included chemo, surgery and radiation.

Katelyn had wanted to do taekwondo since she was about two years old and went with her father and brother to classes. The instructors let her stand in the back of the class and just do what she could, long before she officially started.

In May of 1996, two months after her final chemo treatment, the doctors wired a rod lengthwise through her femur and she wore a leg brace. At this time, Katelyn officially started her training. She would hold onto a wheeled walker and do her kicks. She was five years old.

The summer of 1998 another surgery removed the "hardware," and she wore another leg brace. The doctor was very cautious and feared she would break her leg again. He told her she couldn't play on the school playground or do anything else which might injure her. She wanted to return to taekwondo and did so within two weeks of surgery. We thought this would be good therapy for her leg and help keep her spirits up.

Katelyn was upset whenever she couldn't attend taekwondo classes. If she's held back physically, she finds a way around the problem and accomplishes it. She has learned quite a bit and is currently working towards her high blue belt. We have seen how much she has improved her balance and flexibility. The doctors are impressed with her accomplishments. In fact, one doctor started martial arts lessons because she inspired him.

The taekwondo school has surrounded Katelyn with acceptance, love, support and the same respect and expectations they have for all students. They won't let her feel sorry for herself and haven't felt sorry for her. The school helped raise money to help cover medical expenses. The students of the school also helped raise $1,452 last year for the Children's Miracle Network at the hospital where Katelyn received her care. Katelyn participated in this event as well.

"It's not every day a brother and sister have something in common, especially with our seven year age difference," David said. "She looks up to me, and I help her out as much as she will let me. I admire her because she has courage." ☯

Katelyn's indomitable spirit carried her through many surgeries and treatments with a "can-do" attitude that was encouraged by her family and taekwondo school. In the process, she became an inspiration to others.

Integrity

Integrity is honesty to yourself as well as to others. Everyday Warriors know right from wrong and their actions are the result. Actions they expect of others coincide with actions they expect of themselves. Everyday warriors are trustworthy.

People with integrity fulfill promises they make to others as well as to themselves. They don't pretend, but are honest to themselves and to others. They don't say one thing and do another. And if they promise something, they carry it out.

A person with integrity knows he or she doesn't know everything, is open to learning from others and does so with every opportunity.

Jhoon Rhee

Grand Master Jhoon Rhee is known as the "Father of American Taekwondo" and the inventor of safety gear. Now in his late 60s, Grand Master Rhee can break two boards without spilling a drop from the glass of water balanced on his head.

☯ I believe I must lead by example, by my everyday actions, not just by what I say.

I was in Kustani, Kazakhstan, conducting a seminar to over 3,000 people, including the mayor, the president of the university, professors, students and people from the community. I spoke out against drinking and smoking. That night, I was their guest of honor at a banquet. The mayor started to pour vodka into my glass. I asked him to stop. Since the opportunity had arisen, I asked him some conversational questions.

"Do you have a child?" I asked.

"Yes."

"How old is he?"

"He's 10."

"Is drinking good for your son?" I asked.

"No," the mayor said.

"Does it mean it is good for parents?" I asked.

"No," the mayor answered and called for the audience's attention. "Tonight in honor of Master Rhee, no one is going to drink." And no one did.

We should develop a perfect body to contain a perfect mind. My definition of human perfection is a person who never makes mistakes knowingly, not one who is omnipotent.

Before being honest with other people, I must be honest with myself and responsible to myself. I have to develop knowledge in the mind which means I'm responsible for being reasonably knowledgeable. I also can't make excuses to myself for not having a healthy body.

Every morning, I work out for two to three hours. I have taught taekwondo as a volunteer service to members of Congress, three days a week, for the past 33 years. On the other four mornings, I workout with friends. At first, I arranged things so I couldn't make any excuses for not working out. By inviting my friends the night before, I had to get up and open the door to let them in. Now, I don't need them for the purpose of getting up on time, because it has become a habit to get up early in the morning and exercise. For the past 15 years, I have exercised every day wherever in the world I am, except on the days I'm flying.

Right now, I can sit on the floor, do the splits and touch my chest and lower abdomen flat to the floor. When I was in my 50s, I had lost a lot of the flexibility I had in my youth. When I did this stretch, my chest did not touch the floor. I found that by stretching a little every day, by the end of each month your head will be an inch closer to the floor. At the end of a year, you will improve 12 inches if you stretch every day.

My goal is to achieve 100 years of wisdom in the body of a 21 year old. When I achieve my goal, I would like to share this success with everybody because my success unshared is unfulfilled. ☯

Grand Master Jhoon Rhee is a man of integrity. He knows his weaknesses (such as not wanting to wake up early in the morning) and creatively thinks of ways to strengthen them until they no longer exist as weaknesses, but become strong habits. He lives his life according to his beliefs and makes sure his actions reflect his words.

Bob Wall

In the 1960's, Mr. Wall partnered a chain of schools with Chuck Norris. They were one of the first to open classes to women and children. Mr. Wall has won trophies from major tournaments including the World Karate Championships, the U.S. Nationals, the Tournament of Champions and the Internationals in Long Beach. He had roles in three Bruce Lee movies.

☯ As a kid, I was a wimpy, skinny, weak little geek, and I didn't like it. I was a straight A student in a little country town where everybody admired football, baseball, and basketball players. And I was too small and insecure to play any of them.

My uncle, who had studied judo and karate while serving in military intelligence in Japan, introduced me to the martial arts. I thought it was fantastic. You could break bricks and boards and not be a burly person. But in 1947, there wasn't a karate school in America.

I didn't start taking judo until 1958, when I was a student at San Jose State. I discovered some kung fu schools in San Francisco, but they wouldn't teach me or any other non-Chinese. I finally found a karate teacher in Los Angeles.

I discovered the power of learning, of pushing myself physically. I competed and took first or second in all of the major karate tournaments in the United States. However, I hadn't always won. In fact, I lost all of my fights during my first year-and-a-half of competition. When I started winning, I evaluated why I lost matches and what I was doing differently to win.

With my success, my attitude changed. I no longer had to take any of the malarkey I had taken in the past when I was a geeky kid. It was payback time. Now, with my skills, it was easy to lay everyone else on the ground. I got into a lot of fights out of the competition ring.

One day in the late 1960s, I chased down and beat up two guys who had run a red light and had almost hit the car my wife and I were in.

My wife was furious. "You know, Bob," she said. "You're a punk."

Well, I didn't think so. I had always acted in self-defense. "They all threw the first punches and started the fights," I said.

"Yes. But you're always looking for a problem."

A few days later after thinking hard about what she said, I had to agree with her. After that, I stopped looking for trouble and therefore found a lot less.

I had trained with great martial artists including Chuck Norris, Joe Lewis, Pat Burleson and Bruce Lee. I respected them, not just for their skills but for how they handled themselves personally. They didn't just talk the philosophy, they lived it. I, on the other hand, was tough physically and a geek mentally. It was time to change.

I learned it's not just a high rank or high degree of physical skills that makes a master. It's being able to admit mistakes, learn from them, and demonstrate a good character. ☯

Once Mr. Wall recognized that his actions conflicted with the attitudes he admired in his friends, he had to be honest with himself. He had made a mistake. He didn't give up trying or blame someone else, but took responsibility to change the way he lived his life.

Penny Duggan

Ms. Duggan is a fifth degree Black Belt and a former Midwestern taekwondo champion.

☯ As the highest ranking Black Belt in our taekwondo school, I was given the leadership of the school when Master Yung Sam Kim retired. Even though I had studied with him for almost 20 years, this was not a decision I made lightly.

The night Master Kim announced his retirement, I carefully thought over the implications of taking on the responsibility of being the Master Instructor of his school. I asked for his permission to carry on his teachings, his name and his school and was granted it.

To successfully carry on his traditionally based teachings, it was important for me to involve everyone in our school. I also thought it important to encourage a feeling of loyalty among the black belts to his teachings and traditions. With this loyalty as our base, I wanted to create an environment where everyone had a direct effect on the organization's success by sharing their taekwondo knowledge and skills.

One of the challenges our school faced was how to teach children with Attention Deficit Disorder (ADD). I asked which Black Belt instructors were interested in learning more about ADD. They formed a committee, researched the topic and decided which teaching methods were best. They wrote up their findings and created a document which they presented at a Black Belt meeting. Now all of our instructors know how to teach taekwondo to students diagnosed with ADD. A gratifying result is that our local doctors are recommending our school to their patients with ADD.

We followed the same process to develop self-defense workshops for women and children in the community.

When everyone is involved on a personal level, they take responsibility for the success of a project, whether it be the organization's tournaments, promotion tests, summer camp, or special workshops. ☯

Ms. Duggan showed integrity in following through on her promise to run the school and she showed wisdom by involving all members in the success of the school according to their interests.

Mitch Bartel

Mitch is studying taekwondo.

I was in third grade. My friends and I were going to take a math test, and I had forgotten to study. I was pretty mad at myself. So I tried to do my best and get a good grade.

I got a B-. I was unhappy, because I didn't study. I could have gotten an A. I was happy because I got an okay grade - not a very bad grade - just not the one I wanted.

The next time we had a test, I studied. I tried to study even more because I remembered how I felt when I didn't study last time. ☯

Mitch was honest with himself and took responsibility for his grades and studied to make them better.)

Andy Brown

Mr. Brown is head coach of the Scottish National Team. Taekwondo martial artists in England call him "Mr. Scotland.")

☯ My first experience in the martial arts occurred when I was 14 years old and a friend and his father introduced me to karate. A group of us started training in the local town hall once a week. While it was a brief encounter, it certainly gave me a taste for training.

When I was 16, I learned of taekwondo through an article in a local newspaper. I quickly fell in love with taekwondo, and I soon decided that I must make training a serious part of my life.

There were not many job prospects then for 16 year olds in Scotland. To do taekwondo as a way of life or for a living was quite an impossible idea. However, I had read that if you believe in something enough, then it could be made possible. Taekwondo gave me a purpose when it seemed I had nothing.

I found faith: faith in God, faith in people, faith in the things that you do. I knew I could find success; not success as in how much money I made. Success for me was going to come from within, and martial arts was going to bring it to the surface: the desire to do well, the desire to do the best that I could to improve myself.

At the same time, I realized the importance of helping other people. So whenever my training gave me something of value, I would give it back by helping someone else with their training.

After receiving my Black Belt, I opened a school in Glasgow. I also competed and had to find time to train as well as teach. It was difficult, but teaching is important to me because it builds the future.

One evening, a father brought a very shy seven year old to my school. The father apologized to me saying that his son had asked that he bring him here because he had the crazy notion to join taekwondo. The father said, "I do not expect him to last long training, and I do not want to waste your time, but could you please take him to let him try out taekwondo?" Fifteen years later, that shy seven-year old is a third degree Black Belt and runs that school in Glasgow. ☯

Mr. Brown keeps his promises to himself and to others, doing what he can to further taekwondo in Scotland. Whether he is helping his students become the best they can be, or representing his country in the most ethical and honest way possible, Mr. Brown is an example of integrity in action.

正義

Justice

Some see justice as rather narrow. Justice is outlined by laws a country establishes so that everyone can live in an orderly society.

Yet, rules for living and treating others are not always determined by lawyers. Many actions are based on one's personal moral and ethical beliefs.

Standing up for what you believe is right takes a deep commitment to your personal beliefs. Sticking up for friends and others who are unable to speak up or to protect themselves for whatever reason, requires a steady voice, focused mind, and patience.

Acting for the rights of yourself or another should be done calmly, but forthrightly. By avoiding angry reactions, the other person has to respond to the main point and can't focus on the angry action.

All people have the right to be treated fairly. They should not have to fear violent treatment by neighbors, peers, or their government.

To quote Lucretia Mott: "There can be no true peace without justice."

3

Joe Lewis

Mr. Lewis has won over 30 major titles and was the first martial artist to win world championships in two completely different sports: karate and kickboxing. Mr. Lewis was named to the Who's Who of Martial Arts in 1975. He's never gotten into a fight out of the ring.

Ever since I was 14 years old, I worked out. I lifted weights and wrestled. It wasn't until I was in the Marine Corps in 1962 that I had my first experience with the martial arts. I took my first judo lesson, and I didn't like it.

It took a long time before my attitude changed toward karate. I had a chance to go to Okinawa in 1964, and it was there that I achieved my Black Belt in seven months.

To me, martial arts was a hobby. It was just something I was good at. I enjoyed training. I wanted my body to look good and function at a higher level. It was the challenge of going after this, not titles or trophies. I didn't care about winning. I stayed in the martial arts because it was emotionally rewarding.

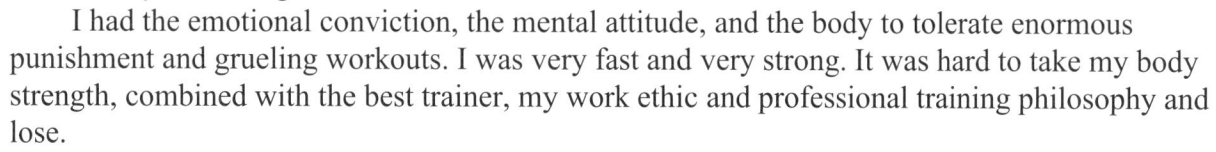

I had the emotional conviction, the mental attitude, and the body to tolerate enormous punishment and grueling workouts. I was very fast and very strong. It was hard to take my body strength, combined with the best trainer, my work ethic and professional training philosophy and lose.

Since I was the top gun, everyone came after me, either attacking me personally or trying to take away my credentials. I didn't pay them any attention.

I strongly believe striking someone out of anger is wrong. Negotiations should be used to remedy a situation, not violence. I still am afraid in some situations, and I still get angry. But it's my nature also to figure out a way to avoid violence and to negotiate a solution.

When somebody jumps in my face, angry and yelling, and wants to fight, I just look him dead in the eye and make a comment which makes him feel like he exists and that someone will listen.

"I can tell you're extremely angry and dying to tear my head off," I say.

The guy just melts inside and agrees with me. I've allowed him to realize that I can see he's emotionally upset, and I don't think there's anything wrong with him being upset.

People should be allowed to express their anger, to talk about what they're upset about.

I was never a little guy. It seems I was always over 200 pounds. I always have had a big brother syndrome, and I still stand up for the people who can't protect themselves.

When I see a parent hitting a child in a grocery store or a bigger person picking on someone smaller, I always step up next to the person being abused. I don't say anything, but I make it clear from my presence, from looking the person in the eye, and saying something non-threatening, that the smaller person has a protector.

My success in the martial arts and my training has enhanced my self-confidence in all parts of my life. This self-assurance goes beyond my skills in karate and kick-boxing and is not limited to knowing I'm good in competition. It permeates my life, helping me make decisions based on what is good for me—personally.

When my wife found a house that cost two-thirds more than what we had been looking at, I said, "I can handle it." My confidence enables me to go after things I want, and make adjustments in my life in order to get them. My success has enabled me to remove the self-centered doubt that says I don't deserve to do something.

Mr. Lewis became the leading fighter because he constantly worked hard. In the process, he learned not to let self-doubt get in his way or to let what others say bother him. He has a strongly developed sense of justice and consistently stands up for people who don't have the power or position to stand up for themselves.

Josh Basile

Josh is a Black Belt in taekwondo.

A kid rode up our alley on his bike and saw me playing basketball on my driveway which faces the alley. He said he knew me from school and bragged about how he was going to steal some lighter fluid and set something on fire. I didn't know whether to believe him or not. I was about 8 years old.

He left, but he soon came back, so I watched him. I saw him go up the alley and soon a flame shot out next to a garage. I watched him run away. I quickly found my Dad, and we told the owner of the garage, who put out the fire.

My Dad and I climbed into our car to search for the boy. When I saw him, Dad got out of the car and held him while someone else called the police. The police found matches in the boy's pocket and arrested him.

We returned with the police to the garage. They said the boy could have caused a really bad fire and burned down the garage.

Following his gut instincts that the boy was telling the truth, Josh stayed watchful, stopped a fire from doing great damage and helped ensure safety in his neighborhood.

Marc Nadeau

Marc has just moved to the Black Belt level in competition. His goal is to be number one in all three of his divisions: forms, weapons and sparring. "I train hard, practice the jumping high kicks in my form, and spar a lot, and I'm slowly creeping up to the others who have been at this level longer."

I always liked the idea of being in karate, but I couldn't join for some time because of my religion. Finally, my father allowed me to do it.

When I first started karate, I acted a lot differently than I do now. I was a little punk. But being around martial artists and seeing how nicely they treated one another and the others around them, grew on me. That and the discipline it teaches.

A year ago, I was walking with my friend at the mall. An older guy, about 22, sitting in a wheelchair was pushed up to us by his friend. He asked me if we wanted some drugs. I said "no" and started walking away. But my friend didn't hear what the man had asked, so he said, "Hold on," and tried to get me to stay. I told him to just come on and pulled him away with me. I described the man to security.

Marc took control of a situation and acted in a manner that kept him and his friend safe. Because he reported the incident, others might be protected from the dealer.

Respect

An Everyday Warrior respects others because of what he or she knows about them, their beliefs and actions. Respect is given based on the personal qualities and actions of the other person.

Respect does not mean blind loyalty to someone just because they are teachers or elders. Respect requires knowledge and thought—Is what the person asking within their rights as a parent, as a teacher, or as an elder? Is what they're asking me to do - good for me? Are they taking good care of me? Are they concerned with my best interests?

When Everyday Warriors respect themselves, they find it easier not to react to other's remarks, name calling and challenges. They find it easier to respect others.

Everyday Warriors respect their physical skills and use them correctly. They don't misuse their skills.

Respect is shown by actions. Everyday Warriors demonstrate respect for themselves and others by doing things such as cleaning their rooms, helping to take care of the yard, doing homework, and taking care of their own toys and property as well as taking care of other people's property.

Everyday Warriors expect to be treated respectfully by others. As one mother stated about the martial arts school her young son attends, "They treat him with respect as the intelligent human being he will become."

Lars Handago

Lars, age 18, studies karate.

☯ When I was younger (about 8 or 9), I briefly trained in the same martial art that I am studying now. I attended classes with my younger sister, who, at the time, had much more patience than I did.

At first I enjoyed class, but soon my interests traveled elsewhere. At one point I was being forced to attend, because I thought there wasn't any application for martial arts in the real world. This was due to a lack of understanding of the knowledge that was being passed on to me. The instructor hadn't made sure I understood what was being taught.

One day I refused to take a class, and he became very impatient with me. I had told him repeatedly that I didn't want to train, but he wouldn't hear of it and tried to shove me into the studio. I was so humiliated that I never wanted to train again.

Years later, one of my friends who was still training brought me to a different karate school. I was still very apprehensive about training again, especially after experiencing first-hand what lack of patience can do for a person. Seeing that this new school was owned by people I knew and trained friends that I hadn't seen in years, I felt an urge to rejoin and begin training again. The new studio provided a non-threatening environment which, to my great relief, taught all their students patience and how to exercise it.

I have studied the martial arts for over six months now and have attended class as often as I can. I had to rebuild all of my basic skills, which meant starting from scratch, but I really didn't mind at all. After school, I try to rush home so I can get to karate as early as I can for three reasons: I love to train even if I am not taking a class, the atmosphere there is very comforting, and I also help out at the Pro-Shop during my spare time.

I am really glad that I gave the martial arts a second chance. ☯

Lars wasn't treated with respect by the instructor. The instructor could command courteous treatment, but not respect. He hadn't earned it. After a few years out of the martial arts, Lars found an instructor who treated him respectfully and a school where he enjoyed training.

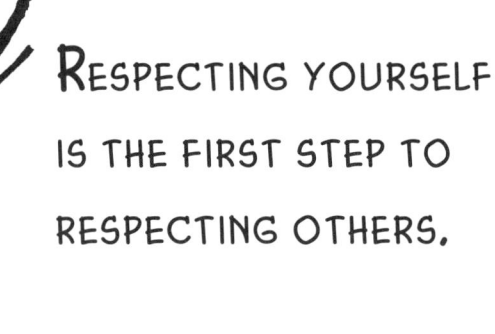

RESPECTING YOURSELF IS THE FIRST STEP TO RESPECTING OTHERS.

Thomas LaPuppet

by Howard Jackson

Thomas LaPuppet, 1938-1999, founded the United Shotokan Association. One of the first major competitors, Mr. LaPuppet competed at both the national and international levels. He is a member of Who's Who in the Martial Arts and the second fighter to be listed in the Black Belt Hall of Fame.

☯ Thomas LaPuppet was a fireman. He related winning to a burning desire in the heart that could never be put out. "As long as the fire burns," he would say, "I can someday attain my goals."

But Tommy knew it takes more than a burning desire to win. He had a lot of respect for himself and for others. He believed strongly that focus and concentration were very important in reaching one's ultimate goals, and that one should never give up until those goals were reached. He helped others find self-respect, achieve their dreams, and feed the fire.

One of Tommy's students was determined to win the AAU Karate Championship, but didn't think he had the potential to do it. Tommy took the student to tournaments and constantly encouraged him, telling him that he could succeed at anything. As the student won more tournaments and moved up in the rankings, his confidence grew. Finally, the student became one of the top fighters in the AAU Karate circuit. ☯

Mr. LaPuppet respected the abilities of his student and helped him achieve his goals. He knew the burning desire was there and that with a little recognition and encouragement, and a lot of hard work, the student would succeed.

Bryan Johnson

(as told by his mother, Lori) Bryan took first place in the NASKA nationals in Las Vegas, Nevada, 1999 in his age and belt division.

☯ My son is a little guy. He is nine years old, weighs 50 pounds and is 3 feet 10 inches" tall. One doctor took one look at him and said, "My God! You're so little!"

People on the streets and in stores looked at Bryan, walked up to us, and said, "You're so cute!" "You're so little!"

These thoughtless remarks hurt Bryan. He would become upset and cry. Size was an issue for him. He often asked me "Why am I so short?" "Will I ever grow?"

But studying taekwondo has given him a new way to look at himself, life and other people. He's no longer intimidated or bothered by rude remarks. Now he smiles and says, "I might be little, but you've never seen me spar."

Bryan carries himself tall and holds his head up. He's proud of himself and people don't see him as "little." He hasn't brought up his size in a year-and-a-half, because it is no longer an issue for him. If he grows to 5'6", 5'9", or even 6', I know he will handle it with grace and dignity. ☯

Bryan respects himself and this self-respect shows in how he walks and handles careless remarks. Because he knows his capabilities, he no longer feels he's limited by his size. Following his example, his mother joined classes. "Taekwondo has given me more respect for myself," she said. "I'm doing things I never did before or even thought of being able to do."

Ryan Smith

Ryan has studied taekwondo for over a year.

What I've learned in class about treating others helps me at school and other places. Now I treat my teachers, friends and other students with more respect and courtesy.

At my school, we have many students with physical and mental disabilities.

One kid in my third grade class sat in a wheelchair. I had to sit next to him everyday. We started talking one day, and we became friends. We liked some of the same things, like cake. He also liked sports like I did, and he wished he could play some.

Later in the year, other kids teased him and I told them to please stop teasing my friend. They stopped.

After learning what perseverance means, I have learned to respect the students with disabilities more, because I can now see how hard it is for them everyday. And they never give up.

Ryan has learned to respect other students for who they are inside, not for how they appear to others.

Ian Hurley

Ian, age 7, is in the first grade. He is a yellow belt studying karate.

I cleaned up my room when my mom didn't ask me. I knew she needed help with the house because my dad was on a trip. I was like the man of the house, and so I did it to help out.

I also take out the trash and the recyclables and my mom only has to ask me once now to do that.

Ian demonstrates respect for his family and for himself by taking care of jobs that need to be done around the house.

Matthew Espinola

As told by Matthew, age 5, and his father Anibal.

I used to get mad and cry when the older kids made fun of me and hurt my feelings.

My Mom suggested I take lessons since I liked the Power Rangers so much, especially the Blue Power Ranger because he has the biggest car.

I just learned the beginning steps of a kata. I practice a lot at home and teach my older sister what I'm learning. I feel good about myself and what I'm learning.

Now when kids make fun of me and wait for me to cry right away, I don't. And they leave me alone.

Respecting himself and feeling good about what he has learned has helped Matthew learn his own strength. He no longer believes those who tease him and can ignore them.

SHOWING RESPECT FOR OTHERS AT HOME AND SCHOOL IS AN IMPORTANT PART OF BEING AN EVERYDAY WARRIOR.

Self-control

    Whatever you say or do, cannot be undone. Everything results in consequences: natural consequences such as failing a test because you didn't study or do the homework or consequences imposed by others such as being grounded for hitting another person. Self-control goes beyond controlling your kicks and punches to controlling your behavior.

    Self-control is patience. Patience with yourself and with what you expect of yourself as well as patience with others and what you expect from them. Patience is when you wait for the right moment to react after assessing the situation. Everyday Warriors don't react impulsively or let anger influence their actions.

    Everyday Warriors control their own actions despite what others are doing. They show self-control. People with self-control don't rely on others to determine their behavior and whether they're good at something. This self-knowledge is not bothered by teasing, by challenges to fight, or by other's beliefs in their abilities. Everyday Warriors know in their hearts who they are and their personal value.

    Everyday Warriors choose not to let others control them and their actions.

Bryan Paris

Bryan, age 12, is a red belt in karate.

I always wanted to train in karate, but I never knew how useful it could be in everyday life.

One time when I was in school, I was really glad that I was a karate student. There was a kid in my middle school who had been bothering me for almost a week and wanted to fight me. Every time he saw me in the hallways, he would shove me up against the wall.

A couple of years ago, I would have gotten into a fight with him, and then I would have gotten into trouble. But since I started training, we had been learning about self-control in my karate class. I wanted to stop the situation without fighting, so I went right up to him and told him to leave me alone or I was going to report him. When he saw that I was not afraid of him, he left me alone.

I'm really glad I handled it that way because nobody got into trouble, nobody got hurt, and my karate instructor was really proud of me when she found out what happened. ☯

Bryan assertively took control of the situation and stopped a person from bothering him. Bryan made sure he wasn't being manipulated into doing something he didn't want to do.

Wendy Langton

Wendy, age 9, is a blue belt, red stripe in taekwondo.

A couple days ago, one of my best friends said she was stupid.

"You're not stupid," I said. She thought I said she was, and she became really mad. I wanted to blow up at her and get really angry.

Instead, I talked to her calmly.

"It was a misunderstanding. I said 'You're not stupid.'"

"Oh, I'm sorry," she said. "I misheard you." ☯

By keeping her temper and watching what she said, Wendy was able to clear up what was said and save the friendship.

David Sleznikow

David is a Black Belt studying taekwondo.

I was very, very nervous when I competed at the Diamond Nationals. It was my first really big tournament, and I really wanted to compete well. I didn't want my nerves to get the best of me.

So, in my mind, I put the matches in perspective. If I lost that was okay, but I had to lose well, not just give up before I even entered the sparring ring. I won my first match and lost my second. But I lost to my opponent, not to myself. I had wanted to compete and I did. I won overall, because I controlled my emotions and my attitude. ☯

By being patient with himself and setting clear goals, David was able to control his emotions and succeed.

Amanda Comminos

Amanda is a yellow belt in karate.

I play many sports including soccer, volleyball and basketball.

The coach of a Club Team saw me playing on a recreational team in our neighborhood and asked my coach if I could be on the Club Team.

There are 18 of us, and we play hard but fair. Not all teams play that way.

In the early spring in an indoor soccer game, members of the other team were tripping people and even slide tackling them from behind. The referee is supposed to call these, but often misses them.

One girl tripped me and slammed me into the wall. I was angry. I could have done the same to her, but it wouldn't do me any good. I controlled my anger and focused on the game. I soon scored a goal. That was far more satisfying than a trip would have been. ☯

Controlling her temper helped Amanda to look for an opening, score a goal and help win the game for her team.

Cody Mann

Cody is a white belt.

I started taking taekwondo because my mother felt I had a violent temper and no self-control. I hit people, often for no real reason.

My instructors talked to me constantly about self-control and the proper use of the martial arts. After six lessons, I walked away from a fight, instead of reacting like I had in the past.

One day at school, I was playing touch football with my classmates. I accidentally ran into a boy and knocked him down. He got mad. "I'll kill you," he threatened.

I walked away. But he tried to grab my neck from behind and scratched it with his fingernails. He was close behind me. So I stepped on his foot and pushed him away and ran. He ran up to me, turned me around and kicked me in the stomach. Still, I showed self-control and left the field to go inside the school rather than fighting and getting kicked out. ☯

Cody is gaining control over his emotions and learning to think of consequences before reacting. In this situation he remained in control and did what he wanted to do, not what the other person wanted him to do.

Adam Paolino

Adam is a Black Belt and studies kenpo karate and Olympic taekwondo. He competes nationally as a member of Team Paul Mitchell. Adam won the NASKA World Championship triple crown in forms, fighting and weapons. In 1998, he also won the NASKA Best Overall Black Belt Boy 17 and Under award.

My mom signed me up for karate lessons seven years ago when I was three, because I was always running around. She said she wanted me to learn something that would help me control my energy.

I found that something in karate. I take lessons almost every day of the week, including private sparring lessons. I think what I do is an art, and I want to express it perfectly, so I practice often.

Karate has helped me control my energy, but I still like to talk a lot. While I'm still very talkative at home, I try not to talk in school and wait until recess to let it out.

Every week in my school, the older students work with the younger students and help them with their math and reading. One afternoon, we went to the auditorium to watch the first graders put on a play. The play was not the most exciting I've ever seen—they were first graders. My friends talked and passed jokes around, and I was tempted to join them. But I didn't. ☯

Adam took the self-control he practiced in tournaments and focused on the reason he was in the auditorium. He didn't want to hurt the feelings of the first-graders and be rude along with his friends. Adam remained in control of himself and his energy.

David Gray

David is an 11 year old Black Belt. He began studying when he was six years old.

I have learned how to be patient and not get really mad as much as I used to do.

I have to teach the PeeWees every Tuesday. They are the kids who are six years old and younger. They don't always listen while I'm teaching. I've learned to say their name, and they look up. Then I have their attention again.

One of the hardest things I've done was test for my Black Belt. It was a three-hour test. We couldn't show any emotions during the test. I made a big mistake in the beginning. I knew it; no one else did. I wanted to cry, but I had to forget the mistake. Before I reached Brown Belt, I probably would have burst into tears and gotten frustrated. But I got myself under control. I kept thinking of my goal, of how nice it would be to have a Black Belt and if I cried, I wouldn't get it. I kept saying "I can do it, I can do it, I cannot cry." And I did well.

It was like during our training. We had to run one and a-half miles. It was hard because I usually don't run long distances. I trained and built up my stamina. A lot of times, I felt like quitting. I focused on the finish line and said, "I can do it" and I ran and tried not to think about running, but about the end. ☯

David has learned to practice self-control when he teaches others and when he, himself, is trying to achieve a goal.

Lisa Conde

Lisa Conde credits taekwondo for teaching her to be alert to her surroundings and the people around her.

Taekwondo taught me to protect myself by thinking smart. As a young, independent woman in a turbulent world, the ability to protect myself is important to me.

One evening, I strolled along the beach alone when I noticed a strange looking man following me. It was just beginning to get dark and people had already begun retiring to their hotel rooms to get ready for dinner and their evening activities.

I was scared and walked immediately to a crowded McDonald's along the strip. I was sure he would disappear once I was near a lot of people.

I entered the ladies room, assuming he would not follow. However, he must have meant to harm me because as I turned on the faucet to wash my hands, he burst into the restroom. As he grabbed my wrist, I took him down in a judo technique which broke his arm. People burst in to investigate the sound of his screaming, not mine.

I felt very proud of myself for preventing what could have been something horrible. I tried to get out of the situation by thinking smart and when that did not help, I resorted to my taekwondo techniques. ☯

Lisa controlled her fear and immediately entered a crowded, well-lit place. When she found that she hadn't removed herself from danger, she used just enough force to protect herself.

Andrew Hoshihara

(As told by his mother) Andrew, 10 years old, is a member of the school's Swat leadership team and Delta team. His goals are to become World Champion, a master instructor, and own his own taekwondo school.)

One evening just before bedtime, Andrew cried and told me he had been picked on by one of his classmates at the Japanese school he attended on Saturdays. I wanted to do something about it, but didn't know what I should do. Andrew has always been well-liked by his classmates so the little incident shocked me. I wanted him to have confidence in himself, so that no matter how other kids would misbehave, he would not be bothered by them.

I signed Andrew up for taekwondo when he was in second grade. He had wanted to earlier, but my image of the martial arts was something "violent." I thought only tall, muscular guys would want to take martial arts lessons.

Now Andrew is in the studio four to five hours every day after school, taking class, assisting the teacher or practicing his forms. He does his homework right away so he can go to class.

While there are those who still do things that aren't pleasant to him or to his friends, now he knows that he has no control over how other kids behave, but he himself can make a big difference no matter how others behave. When he or a friend is mistreated, he speaks up and says, "What if you're the one who is treated like this? How would you feel?"

Andrew always makes friends at tournaments. Many of the kids who Andrew competed with in the past come to his ring to vigorously cheer him. When you respect people, they do the same in return. Andrew is only ten years old, but he knows that. ☯

Learning to focus and control his energy, has helped Andrew do well both in school and in taekwondo. This confidence has improved his self-control, and he now politely and effectively confronts those who mistreat him or his friends.

Theresa Hunter

Theresa is a Black Belt in taekwondo and a Religious Studies major at St. Norbert College.

I am an intern in our junior high and high school youth program at church. For the past year in addition to being a full-time college student, I assisted our Youth Director. I help plan Wednesday night programs for both groups, am the main leader for the junior high youth group, co-teach junior high Sunday School, help make arrangements for our groups to attend state-wide convocations, help write and layout articles for the monthly newsletter, help set up weekend retreats and many other activities involved in running a successful youth program.

Late one afternoon after I raced from the college campus to church, I discovered my computer files had accidentally been deleted.

I was devastated. A year's work, the basis of my portfolio, ideas which could be altered or used again in my future work as a youth leader, were erased. I hadn't kept hard copies, and I hadn't saved my files on a separate disk.

It was almost time for the Wednesday evening programs to start. I had to control my frustration and disappointment and focus on the students in my care.

I made it through the evening. The students didn't know I had a problem.

Luckily, a computer wiz at our church was able to rescue most of my files. And I've learned to save my files on a separate disk and run-off hard copies. ☯

By controlling her frustration, Theresa handled the evening's classes professionally. She realized that focusing her energy on her students was her first responsibility.

Jeremy Langton

Jeremy is a red belt, black stripe in taekwondo. He is 11 years old.

I was talking with my friend in our neighborhood one evening around 5 p.m.
A kid walked by and called my friend "a wimp."
"A wimp is one who can't control themselves," I said.
"Are you calling me a wimp?" he asked.
"No. But if you punch me now you will be."
He looked disgusted, but he walked away. ☯

Jeremy could have reacted differently and kicked or punched the boy, but that would have made things worse. By showing self-control, Jeremy handled the situation well and didn't let his behavior be controlled by the boy.

J.P. Roeske

J.P. is the 1995 NASKA - North American Karate Association - National Champion and Youth Overall Forms Champion. From 1996 to 1998, he was the National Champion and World Champion. His television and movie credits include 3 Ninjas - High Noon at Mega Mountain, Saved by the Bell, *and* Profiler *and he has done commercials for Pizza Hut and McDonald's.*

I have practiced martial arts since I could walk. My parents are instructors. I went to my first tournament when I was three years old. I won my first national championship when I was five.

Because of my success at such an early age, newspapers, magazines and talk shows were interested in doing stories about me.

One thing led to another, and I moved from Wisconsin to California. A talent agent sent me out on auditions.

After a few auditions and acting classes, I booked the role of "Tum Tum" in *3 Ninjas - High Noon at Mega Mountain*. Several commercials and television guest spots followed.

Auditions can be very tense at times, because there might be 100 kids trying out for the same role and everyone wants it. That is when I depend on the confidence I've developed, on my patience and perseverance.

On many of the jobs I booked, the directors and producers told me that I have more discipline than other kids they've worked with.

I tell them it's because of my martial arts training. I plan to continue to use my martial arts skills in my acting career and whatever else I choose to do.

J.P.'s ability to control his actions and follow directions has led to a good reputation in the movie industry.

Anthony Carrasco

Anthony is a high red belt in taekwondo.

My school shares a bus with the private school across the street. Three of the older kids from that school would get on the bus and pick on me, calling me names.

I've been in taekwondo for four years now. I know that taekwondo is used for protection when someone is physically threatening me. In this case, I didn't need to use unnecessary violence.

I had just sat down when they climbed on the bus, walked back to where I was and began hassling me. I kept them away from me by using my feet to block them. I reported the incident, and the principals from the two schools took care of it. The principal told my mother how pleased he was with the self-discipline I showed in handling this incident.

Anthony gained the confidence he needed to do only what was necessary to control the situation.

Micah O'Malley

Mr. O'Malley is a second degree Black Belt in aikido. He started when he was 15 years old after his sister had been taking for a year.

☯ My sister had a lot of fun in aikido. Whenever she returned from class, she'd walk through the house searching for one of us to practice on.

"Grab my wrist, you big bully," she always said, sticking her wrist out. We were supposed to grab it, and she would use some kind of a twist to get free.

Her phrase became a family joke, especially in reference to me. I was not a bully. I stayed away from all fights and arguments. I never confronted anybody when I was growing up. I remember being uncomfortable around strong emotions, particularly anger, even if they weren't directed at me.

My sister's interest fanned my and our mother's interest, and we also took lessons. They stopped, but I continued and even started an aikido club when I moved to a town without one.

After studying aikido for several years, I attended an aikido seminar in New York city. I had to take the subway, and it was late at night.

Only myself and one other person were in the car. I sat, and he stood.

"Do you have a dollar I can hold?" he asked.

People have asked me for handouts before. This felt different. It felt like some weird game. What was I supposed to do? Give him the dollar to hold and then ask for it back?

The atmosphere in the car was most uncomfortable.

I looked him calmly in the eye and said, "No."

We maintained eye contact until the next stop when he got off. ☯

Mr. O'Malley assessed the situation, showed self-control and didn't overreact. By staying calm and controlling his own actions, Mr. O'Malley controlled the other person's actions. As a side note: Mr. O'Malley said that his sister hasn't asked him to grab her wrist for a really long time. "I now know the techniques better than she does," he said.

Kevin Thomas Castle

Kevin is 11 years old and a yellow belt in kempo karate.

We played basketball in gym class. At the last minute, I dribbled the ball away from the guy who was guarding me, moved to a good position and shot the winning basket. He was mad. "I'm going to beat you up after school," he said. My karate instructor always told us to just get out of the way if someone tried to hit us. I remembered that when I ran into the guy after school. He tried to punch me, and I moved out of the way. He tried to punch me again, and again. I just moved out of the way. Five times he tried to punch me before he fell down on his face, and I left.

Kevin followed his teacher's advice and moved out of the way until finally the attacker lost his balance and fell over. Kevin stayed calm and kept his emotions under control.

Nicky Natalino

Nicky, 8 years old, is a Black Belt in taekwondo. He began studying just before he turned 6 years old.

I do better in my classes now. Before, if something was difficult to learn or do, I used to quit. I would say, "I can't do that," or "I'm not going to try it today."

Now, when I have a hard problem, I try to figure it out. My subtracting improved because I practiced at home, at a friend's house, on a park bench, in the car and at school.

My handwriting is better because I'm taking the time to practice it and my spelling has improved.

I run up to the teacher's desk less often. I raise my hand when I have to ask my teacher a question, and only go up to the desk when I really need to. ☯

By sticking with a hard task instead of quitting, Nicky improved his grades. He also gained more self-control in the classroom.

Ryan Hurley

Ryan, 6 years old, is in kindergarten. He is a yellow belt in kempo karate.

I have a bad temper. My mom says I used to get angry really quickly. Sometimes I would hit back. I have learned to count to ten before I react.

My youngest sister is almost two years old. The other day, she bit me. She was playing with something that could hurt her, and my mom had asked me to take it away. When I did, my sister got angry and bit me. Long ago, I would have bitten her back. This time, I closed my eyes and counted to ten. This gave me time to calm down. ☯

By practicing self-control and counting to ten before he reacts, Ryan is accepting responsibility for his behavior and making sure he doesn't hurt others.

Patricia Wilson

Patricia is a 10 year old Black Belt.

In school, I was given an independent research assignment on the Mississippi Valley Indians and Mound Builders. I started working on it right away. We had some time to do it in class, but not enough. I didn't fool around after school with my friends, and I worked hard on it every day, even on weekends.

I finished before everyone else. My friends were shocked that it was done. They said, "I barely have it started!"

I felt good because I didn't have to worry about it anymore. ☯

Patricia tackled the assignment right away when she still had plenty of time to do it. This kept it from becoming a huge, last minute project.

Harrison Schultz

Harrison Schultz is part Native American, growing up in a predominantly white city in the Midwest. He and his mother began studying taekwondo when Harrison was five. He recently was inducted into the National Honor Society.

The taekwondo school was the one place in my town that I could go where I felt like I could be accepted and respected by people my own age and by adults.

When I was younger, I had bragged a lot about taking the martial arts and it got me into trouble. I hadn't really cared about becoming as good at taekwondo as I could have. It had just been an interesting thing to do. I wanted to quit soon after receiving my probationary Black Belt, but my parents wanted me to continue so I waited to quit until after I achieved my Black Belt.

After getting my Black Belt, I was beaten up by someone who I believed was my friend. I thought we were just playing around. My friends and classmates who knew I was a Black Belt, never let me forget it.

Even though I wasn't studying taekwondo, I still kept in contact with my instructor. Now and then I would help him clean the studio for a little extra spending money. One day I noticed a pile of wooden practice swords stacked in a corner. I had never had a chance to learn the sword when I was younger. So I asked him if I could exchange cleaning for sword lessons. It took only one lesson for me to regain my interest in the martial arts.

This time around I studied really hard. I practiced zealously for over a year, and I tested successfully for my second degree Black Belt. It takes a great deal of interest and devotion to become good at something.

Since I started studying taekwondo again, I haven't gotten into any physical confrontations. I don't feel the need to talk to anyone about my skills unless they are interested in the martial arts. ☯

Everyday Warriors don't brag about accomplishments, because they are confident in themselves. As the martial arts became more and more a part of who Harrison is as a person, his self-confidence grew and he felt he didn't have to talk about what he had accomplished. He has become calmer and more in control of himself.

Joseph Mora

Joseph began studying taekwondo when he was almost 7 years old. His role model is his teacher. "She is tough but fair."

Everyday at school a boy pushed me out of line, again and again. I was getting tired of it, so one day I pushed him back. He hit me in the stomach and knocked me down.

I didn't do anything though I wanted to hit him back. He got into trouble, and I didn't. I didn't want to get suspended because that is the rule at our school if we fight.

Afterwards, I told him that if he ever touched me again I would have to defend myself. I felt like a winner. I hadn't used my karate skills on him because I had too much to lose. Fighting is the easy way out. I felt very good when I reasoned with him. ☯

Joseph's self-control stopped him from hitting the boy back and turning a small incident into a larger one. His self-control also helped him talk calmly to the boy and tell him never to push him again and thus ended the pushing.

Ken Martin

Ken is a brown belt.

At football practice, we ran plays with the offense going live (full contact) against the defense. I played offense and was lined up over the defensive tackle. When the ball was snapped, I drove the tackle backwards. Soon after, he seemed to give up. Seizing the chance, I got under his shoulder pads and tossed him into the air, landing him on his back. The whistle blew and ended the play.

But he was angry. I could see in his eyes he wanted to hurt me, and I prepared for the attack. He charged me with closed fists. I dodged his punches to my head and stomach and threw him to the ground. By then, the other players had noticed and kept him from attacking me anymore.

I was angry and confused. I was shocked at his sudden outburst because it was a fair hit. I regained focus in the huddle and was glad that I kept the situation from escalating by using self-defense.

Later, I talked with him to find out why he had gotten so angry. He said that when I blocked him, he thought he heard the whistle so he stopped hitting. When I knocked him down, he thought I was cheating so he lost control. He apologized, and I accepted. I think that without the training I received from the martial arts, I wouldn't have handled that situation as well.

By using self-control, Ken kept a bad situation from developing into something worse.

Jacob "Jake" Fischer

Jake, a Black Belt, began studying karate almost four years ago.

I was always getting picked on in school, and it made me angry. I stopped talking to anyone but my friends, and we were always getting into trouble.

As I progressed from belt to belt, I became smarter and learned more control. I hang out now with a different set of friends.

One day after I'd been in karate awhile, one of my friends came to my karate class to watch me work out. He saw me sparring. Later a rumor went around school about how I could beat up everyone, and people stopped making fun of me. My anger dropped to nothing.

I concentrate better in school and my grades are up. In science class our teacher lectures one day and gives us a quiz the next day. He doesn't tell us exactly what will be on the quiz, so I have to listen really well to his talks, take good notes and study. If I didn't, I wouldn't get good grades.

One night, one of my friends tried to get me to sneak out of the house and go to a block party. I said no, because I didn't want to get into trouble. So he spent the night at my house, and we went skateboarding.

By applying the skills he had learned in karate to his study habits, Jake's grades improved. By demonstrating his abilities in a non-threatening atmosphere, the word got out that he knew how to fight. People left him alone. He felt less angry, more in control of himself, and able to make good decisions for himself and his friends.

Wisdom

Everyday Warriors demonstrate wisdom when their actions are based on their sense of justice and knowledge of right and wrong. Wisdom comes from experience and from studying. Wisdom is taking care of things, whether it will be a great accomplishment or a problem, while they are still small. It's easier to study for a test over a period of time than to cram it all in at the last minute.

One part of wisdom is knowing when to fight and whom to fight. Everyday Warriors judge each situation. They never use their power or strength without wisdom.

True wisdom comes from knowing oneself as well as others with whom one is dealing with. Like the Boy Scouts' motto, "Be Prepared," martial artists are alert to what is happening around them. Being aware allows the Everyday Warrior to adapt to different situations.

The Everyday Warrior is well-rounded. In addition to physical skills, the Everyday Warrior reads, plays instruments, and has many interests. Everyday Warriors apply the knowledge gained from the martial arts to other activities. For instance, the moves of aikido can be applied to the game of basketball, or the strategies of a champion fighter can be applied to relationships.

Ernie Reyes Jr.

Ernie Reyes, Jr., was 8 years old when he first competed and won against adults. His movie roles include Last Dragon, Red Sonja *with Arnold Schwarzenegger,* Teenage Mutant Ninja Turtles I and II, Surf Ninjas *and some serials for Disney.*

☯ When I was little, I walked home from school with my head down, looking at the cracks in the cement and watching my feet step forward, first one then the other. Time had no meaning. Before I knew it, I raised my head and I was home.

Life for me has been like that. I put my head down and do the work and before I know it, I am there.

My father began training me in the martial arts when I was seven. I worked out before school, went to school, came home, ate, and then worked out some more. I just accepted it. Working out was my way of life. I didn't care about competing nationally. And yet within one year, I was competing professionally against adults.

Twenty years later, I can look back to my childhood and I can see how my growing up in the martial arts has affected my day to day living. I've learned life is a process. It is meant to be lived, not hurried through.

I have just begun to scratch the surface of my understanding of the martial arts and the benefits I've gained by living the martial arts the way that I have.

When I don't worry about time or how long something will take to accomplish, I have all the time I want. I become time's master, rather than time deciding for me what will be done. Sometimes, when people start thinking about how many years it will take to reach their goal, they quit before they even begin.

Just as I trained constantly and won national competitions when I was younger, I now 'train' and do activities to help make me a better actor, director, writer and martial artist.

As an actor, I do various relaxation, creation and imagination exercises. I read plays, rehearse speeches, and read books about acting by major teachers in the world. To prepare myself as a writer, I read books about writing by the greatest playwrights and dramatists, as well as plays by Moliere, Shakespeare, the Greeks and Ibsen. I write every day.

To become a better director, I direct a scene, read the writings of and watch movies by directors such as Kurosawa, Fellini, and Bergman.

As a martial artist, I exercise three to five hours a day, doing stretching, conditioning techniques and cardiovascular exercises.

I have found the joy of living comes from my being anchored in the martial arts and my discovery that life is a process. When many in the western world try to short cut the process, they increase their stress and anxiety. I gain freedom through the discipline of 'doing and being' the person I want to become.

One day I'll look up, and I'll be there. ☯

Mr. Reyes continues to live, work and study hard to be the person he intends to be. He has achieved much by being totally committed to each experience.

Gokor Chivichyan

Mr. Chivichyan is the 1997 Black Belt Hall of Fame "Judo Instructor of the Year."

☯ I started studying sambo, which is a lot like judo and wrestling, when I was five years old. I remember what it was like to train and work hard to be a member of a team when I was so young. I still remember what motivated me. Training was fun. As I grew older and better in the sport, I also liked practicing what I wanted to work on and working out with a partner I chose rather than what and who my teacher had selected.

My goal as a teacher today is to build my students' motivation, to create in them a good attitude and a love of the sport.

Many of the children are happy and can't wait to come to class. They are faster and train harder.

Others who are there because their parents pushed them are slower and really don't want to train.

To change the attitudes of those who don't want to be there, I turn the training into games and make it fun.

For instance, instead of ordering them to run, I ask them "Who can be the first to touch the wall?" Even the lazy student wants to win a game and starts running hard.

When we do push-ups, I ask who can do more when they get to a certain point. I turn it into a fun challenge. Someone who usually finds it hard to do 40 push-ups, will do 300 if it's a game because they want to keep up with the others.

Making training fun for the students is a good way to motivate them. Just because something is fun, doesn't mean it's not helping them to grow stronger and faster. People train harder when they love the sport.

I have found that it usually averages two months for students with bad attitudes to change and grow to love the sport. Then they are ready to train hard.

In one case, a student with a poor, know-it-all attitude came to the school. He was very disrespectful and didn't think much of what we did. I didn't get mad and demand respect. I took him aside and put him into a few holds from which he couldn't escape. Then I taught him moves that would get him out of those holds. He had a good time and learned the value of studying judo. He left the studio feeling good and wanting to come back for more.

My students must be humble. To be one of the best, they have to be willing to learn from others and be a loveable person, not a braggart. They thank all of their opponents, whether they have won or lost because there is something they can learn from each match and I want them to remain open to learning.

I believe that what I teach is so important that I'm willing to make it fun and challenging so people will learn. Just because something is fun to learn does not mean it's not serious. ☯

Mr. Chivichyan hasn't forgotten what it is like to be young and remembers what motivated him to keep training. He creatively thinks of ways to make training fun, to teach his students the meaning of respect, and create in them a desire to succeed.

Bruce Lee

by Pat Burleson

One of the best known martial artists, Bruce Lee's legacy lives on in his movies and in memories of those who knew him. He was one of the first to take stylized fighting techniques and adjust them to practical situations. This resulted in the creation of Jeet Kune Do.

☯ One of Bruce Lee's passions was movies. He liked to go to China Town in Los Angeles and watch samurai movies.

I would work out for two hours with Bruce in his garage in central Los Angeles and then we would go the movies in China Town. I knew whenever I worked out with Bruce, I'd blow a whole day.

Bruce was in the *Green Hornet*, and passersby on the street were beginning to recognize him. He was often challenged, but he always declined the challenges.

One time after we left the movie theatre, I noticed some gang bangers gathering ahead of us. Bruce was talking to me about something in the movie and gave no indication he saw these guys. I watched them circling us, positioning themselves.

By the time Bruce gave any recognition of their presence, we were surrounded.

The leader approached us, flanked by a couple of his guys. He talked tough to Bruce, saying Bruce did things on TV, but the leader doubted Bruce could do anything effective on the street.

It looked to me that the situation was rapidly getting bad. It would not be long before the talking would stop, and they would attack. So I punched the leader and took him out and reached around for the second person. Then the whole gang ran.

I thought I had done pretty well.

"Why did you hit him?" Bruce asked.

Bruce was definitely the teacher, and I deferred to him. "I hit him because I have found it's easier to stop a situation before it blows up in your face. If you take the leader out, the others fold."

I also thought they would take out knives soon and someone would get cut because they had us circled. I didn't tell him I was worried about him getting hurt.

Bruce gave me a big speech on not paying attention to the situation and overreacting.

"The way the guy was standing was a clear indication that he didn't want to fight," Bruce said. "He just wanted to talk. If he had changed stances, I would have taken him out before you even moved."

I got an object lesson that day. I call it "Saving Bruce Lee from getting into a street fight." Bruce called it "Overreaction." ☯

Bruce Lee demonstrated wisdom in judging the situation and realizing fighting wasn't necessary.

Pat Burleson

Mr. Burleson combined moves from many arts into what he calls American Karate. He won the first United States National Karate Championships. He has appeared in many episodes of Chuck Norris' Walker, Texas Ranger series, as well as a few of his movies including Sidekicks.

☯ I joined the U.S. Navy Special Forces in the late 1950s. As I traveled around the Pacific Basin with the military, I studied various fighting systems from China, Japan and Korea.

At that time, martial arts teachers were not easy to find, even in Asia. It was generally a skill that was passed from one family member to another. In Japan, I searched until I learned of a skilled man who lived on the seashore. Again and again, I approached him and finally convinced him to teach me.

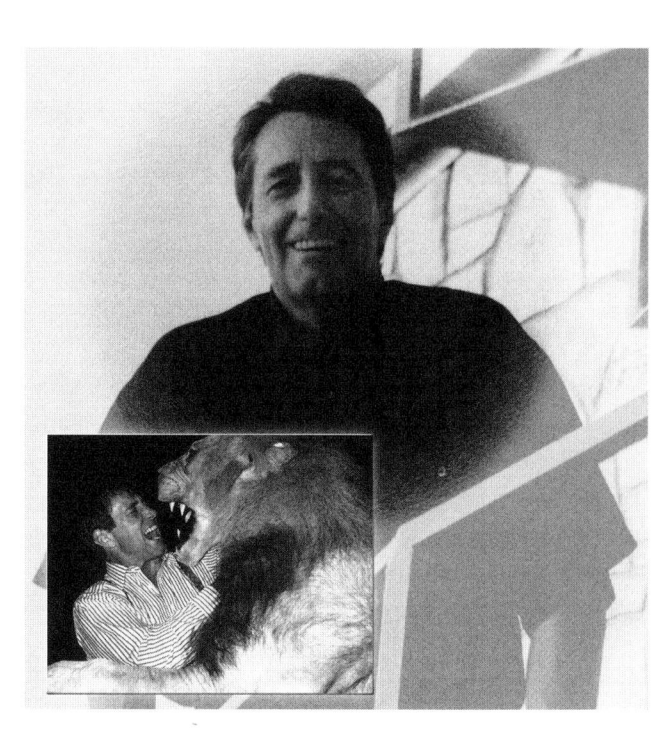

I am one of the original pioneers who brought martial arts to the United States. We were an elite group and walked around with the attitude, "I can't be beat." We fought hard and taught hard. At that time, competition was semi-full contact with no gloves. This meant bare knuckles, kicks, throws, etc.

Because someone was always getting hurt, karate was only taught to males who were in their late teens or early 20s. Our attitude wasn't all right, but through us, karate gained enormous respect and popularity and began to appear in movies. Schools opened by the thousands in American cities across the United States.

I had opportunities through Chuck Norris and Bruce Lee to appear in some of these early movies. The first one that Chuck and I did was a Dean Martin private detective movie. Whenever they used martial arts moves, Chuck and I yelled for the background "kiai." I also did stunt work for *Black Belt Jones*, but didn't go further then into an acting career because I preferred teaching and being with my family.

In the late 1980's, I talked with a behavior moderationist and co-founded an international children's character building program. I call it YES (Youth Enrichment Skills). It forms the basis of my karate classes. When children first come in, their first earned stripe is for behavior. I teach them how to apply the self-control and self-discovery they learn in karate to their behavior at home and in the classroom.

I use the self-control I perfected while studying the martial arts in my everyday conversations, especially when how I say something may result in losing or retaining a friend. This is strategy: stopping, thinking, and responding with a planned reaction rather than inappropriate aggressiveness and anger. I end up with better results if I think before I respond.

In the past few years, I've produced a series of instructional videos and have given karate related seminars around the world. My life changed because I was willing to listen and implement what I learned from others. ☯

Mr. Burleson adapted his teaching style because of an overheard conversation. He was wise enough to thoughtfully consider what he was doing, to ask advice and to create a system that deliberately helps others develop good character traits.

Robert Halstead

Robert is a 13 year old red belt, studying free-style united arts.

I'm usually one of the last people to leave the locker room after gym class.

One afternoon, there was only one other person and myself left in the room. He lit a cigarette.

I told him that smoking was bad for him, but that if he was going to smoke, he should do it some place else rather than on school grounds where it was banned.

"Do you want one?" he asked.

When I said, "No," he threatened to hurt me if I told anyone he was smoking. I told him that I wasn't going to say anything, and I left.

But smoke had seeped out of the room, and he was caught. He thought I had ratted on him.

He waited for me after school and a lot of kids were around him. He accused me of telling. I told him that I hadn't said anything, and I calmly walked away. He didn't come after me or anything.

Robert's actions were based on his sense of right and wrong. He looked at the pros and cons and made a decision not to smoke. Confident that he had made the right decision for himself, he could respond with courtesy and certainty to the boy when he later accused Robert of ratting.

Alexander Koborov

Mr. Korobov teaches taekwondo in the country of Ukraine. His studio, "School of Leaders," has two gyms and an office in the State Children Palace building. A former professor of economics at Kiev University, he is now a "professor" in his own studio.

I started a new educational system in my country. After studying the martial arts for 16 years, I received an invitation from the Philosophical Society of the USSR to attend a Jhoon Rhee Seminar in Moscow. They were promoting martial arts as education. I hadn't thought of that idea before.

It was a challenge. I invited two instructors from Russia to Kiev and suggested we try to work together. In one year, we gave hundreds of classes in different places to more than 10,000 children. Once the government gave us the go-ahead on this new system, we started 10 studios, and I moved temporarily to the United States to learn more. Three years later, my two Russian friends had to return to Russia. By this time, I had other instructors and the school was a success.

Students at my school receive an education that goes beyond the kicks and punches of taekwondo. My students learn English, French, philosophy, economics and physical fitness. And my family has benefited. I had learned about balance. I found that I was like many martial artists. I practiced and practiced martial arts, and even though I learned more, my life didn't change. It wasn't balanced. So I changed my life. I now spend time with my family too.

Mr. Korobov lives a life of balance, spending time at his martial arts school and with his family. His students study many subjects so they can grow into balanced, global citizens and be successful in their daily lives.

Joshua William Benner Fox

Joshua studies karate and is a Black Belt.

My band teacher asked me to switch from bass clarinet to tenor saxophone, because one of the other students could not play high notes. It was really hard for me to do, because I had to learn to play a new instrument after just learning to play the bass clarinet. But I didn't want to tell him that and not even try to learn. I'm now one of the two members of our band who can play tenor sax. And now I can play three different instruments (clarinet, bass clarinet and tenor sax.)

As I learned to be a Black Belt, it taught me to be a better student also.

Joshua's self-confidence grew as he learned more skills in karate. He transferred this confidence and in the process has gained new skills in other areas of his life.

Sean Stephen Castle

Sean, 12, is a yellow belt studying kempo karate.

My self-discipline has improved, especially in school. I'm doing better and bringing homework home. I take notes in class, study them and reread the chapter to help me memorize the information before a test.

The last test I took, which covered angles, was really easy. But I had prepared well for it.

Sean had a test coming up and showed wisdom in preparing for it one step at a time. Because he had really learned the information, the test was "easy."

Jessica Peck

Jessica studies taekwondo.

My Dad is in the United States Navy. He traveled a lot when I was young. When I turned ten, he was permanently stationed in our city. For three months, I watched him leave the house and go to taekwondo classes. Then for three more, I watched as my younger sister left with him to go to taekwondo. So I joined so I could have more chances to spend time with my Dad.

Now that I'm a teenager, I take the same classes as my Dad. I used to help him teach. Now we teach different classes.

We also compete. We traveled to Washington D.C. to Jhoon Rhee's convention and tournament where I was certified as a Black Belt instructor. This was a trip we wouldn't have taken unless we were both involved in the martial arts.

I've gained plenty of quality father/daughter time with my Dad and opportunities to talk about life. It helps keep our lines of communication open.

I'm making more A's in school because I'm studying better for my classes. My taekwondo instructor has helped me think more creatively. He converts dry information that is really boring into ways that make me interested. To help me study for a science test on chemicals, equation and balance, my instructor turned the information into a song. I really like to sing, so I was able to memorize it quickly and easily.

Jessica decided she wanted more time with her father and chose taekwondo and laid the groundwork for them to continue to talk and share experiences as she grows older. She has also learned that boring material can be made interesting and memorable.

集中

Focus

Focus is the controlled, calm center that can be found in everyone. When a person is distracted by thoughts or another's actions, the person's attention wanders from the job at hand. What the person is trying to accomplish suddenly gets only half-done because full attention is not being paid to it.

Everyday Warriors increase their chances for success by focusing on one thing at a time. They don't allow other thoughts or people to distract them from their goals.

When Everyday Warriors focus on one thing, their attention should be backed by good intentions and not be entirely self-serving.

Marti Freund

Marti is 9 years old and a Black Belt. She started studying karate when she was five.

This summer, I took football for three weeks. I had never been very good at catching balls. One day, the ball was coming toward me. My first thought was "I can't do this." Then I remembered my Black Belt and all the things I had found out that I could do. So I said, "I can do it." I focused hard on the ball, and I caught it. ☯

Marti took the self-confidence she gained from karate and applied it to other parts of her life. The thought that she could do it, helped keep her calm and focused on the ball.

Luke Boucher

Luke is a second level brown belt. Now in the eighth grade, Luke has studied shotokan karate and jiu-jitsu for the past six years.

Taking the martial arts has helped me learn how to focus on what I want to do and not join the crowd.

In English class, the teacher was trying to explain something while many of the students around me talked and made jokes. They wanted me to laugh too, and I told them to leave me alone. I didn't want to get into trouble. They eventually left me alone when they found they couldn't get my attention. ☯

Focusing can take many forms. What an Everyday Warrior does can affect many other people. That is why it is important to keep one's goals in sight.

Julia Krasovskaia

Julia is a Black Belt. She is 14 years old and studies taekwondo in the country of Ukraine. Julia would like to enroll in a good university.

In 1998, I had some problems with my classmates. They asked me to go away from their class. Everyday, I heard chattering and laughing behind my back. I felt awful.

I made myself ignore them and think only about my studies. As a result, I had better grades at the end of the year.

And I must say that my classmates began to respect me, because they understood that I was stronger than they thought.

If I want my life to be better, I must do better myself. We all have troubles everyday. I am not afraid of them and that's why my life becomes better and better with each day. ☯

Julia focused on her studies and ignored the classmates who teased her. She didn't allow herself to be distracted by them. In the end, she accomplished two things. Her grades improved and she gained the respect of her classmates.

Matt Hawkinson

Matt studies taekwondo and is a Black Belt.

When I was 10 1/2 years old, I was in the hospital for a week for treatment of an illness located behind my eye. I had IVs, a lot of tests and surgery. I went home and for the next eight weeks was hooked up to a special IV and took antibiotics.

I had to focus on not feeling pain, otherwise the IVs, tests and surgery would really hurt. So I used the meditation techniques I learned in class to clear my mind and relax.

I have been in taekwondo for four years. Before every class, we close our eyes and relax for about 30 to 40 seconds. We think about what we're going to do in class. After the class, we meditate again to review in our minds what we did in class.

I really believe the meditation techniques helped me get through this experience. ☯

Matt found his calm center through the meditation techniques he had learned in class and was able to focus on not feeling pain.

Michael Cartwright

Six years ago when he was four, Michael began studying karate. His favorite aspect is competition, especially the areas of sparring and traditional kata. He trains every day. His personal goal is to win the NASKA World Championship. He never talks about his karate accomplishments at school. His school work, which he does well, comes first.

This year, I am competing in NASKA tournaments in almost every state. I'm even going to an international tournament in Toronto.

I like to compete, but a lot of times people go crazy at competitions. Not the competitors, but their parents. It makes me just want to get out of there, but I remember my goal.

At the USA Nationals in Las Vegas, the tournament was held in a large hotel with lots of people, lots of noise and many competition rings.

I fought five fights that day. Right before one of my fights, a kid drew blood from his opponent. The head judge said it was a hit to the shoulder. The other two judges said the boy had hit the opponent's nose.

The mother of the boy who was hurt got really angry. They called an arbitrator who said that if the head judge hadn't seen the illegal contact then the fight would continue.

The mother yelled at her son to go over and hurt the other kid. After her son lost, it was my turn to fight the winner.

She started screaming at me. "Go stick your foot in his face. Go hurt him!"

I just tried to focus and concentrate on the fight and not on her negative, distracting talk.

I won fairly, and his mother didn't do much after that. The next round was the finals, and I won. ☯

Michael has learned the value of focusing on his opponent and ignoring distractions. He keeps his goal and the desire to win fairly in sight.

Christy Fink

Now a Black Belt, Christy attended an introductory taekwondo class with two of her girlfriends and liked it so much she chose martial arts over dance lessons.

At age 10, I was very shy and uncomfortable talking with adults and with other kids I didn't know that well. I also had a hard time standing and talking in front of the classroom. I was easily sidetracked by everything around me and the doctors thought it might be ADD (Attention Deficit Disorder), as well as signs of dyslexia.

I am a junior in high school now, and I do a lot of acting. In order to get a job, I have to audition for the part.

I recently auditioned for a car commercial. Many people stood around watching and judging how good I was. There were the director and people from the ad agency, the camera crew and many more. All of the others who were trying out for the same job could see and hear me through the windows.

I was given my lines and a few minutes to practice. I thought about what I was doing and focused my energies as I had learned in taekwondo. Then I stood in front of everyone and the camera and confidently delivered my lines.

I know who I am at this point in my life, and I like who I am. I don't have to prove anything to anyone else. If, however, they have a problem with me, I'm willing to listen. ☯

Studying the martial arts has made a big difference in Christy's life, building her self-confidence and teaching her to focus on what she is doing and to ignore distractions.

HAVING FOCUS IN TOUGH SITUATIONS CAN MEAN THE DIFFERENCE BETWEEN SUCCEEDING AND FAILING.

Everyday Warriors

My son is now ... a third dan in taekwondo ... a nine year old whi... ...ing mom," one ... sit outside the ... ...eir kids are in ...

... martial arts for man... too old to start. I had a... ...ional and national trade magazines, b... ... written. After all, I was a "sitting mo... ...d learn, but I was already an adult. W... ...do?

Well, I started classes, wit... ...ooked like such fun. I found I loved ... ...n't a "sitting mom" any longer.

I have achieved second dan, ... am honored to know Everyday Warri... ... of life, and from around the world.

Every day, what I learn from m... on my life.

All martial artists are connected. ... skills and develop ourselves.

To be our best, we all must train, w... ...e all must teach, and we all must operate out of the c... ...ther that our history and tradition dictates.

Everyone can become an Everyday Warrior. It takes practice. It takes thought. It is in each of us to use what we learn to become better people.

When we do this, we inspire each other, regardless of our age or experience.

Are You an Everyday Warrior?

All of the martial artists in this book are Everyday Warriors, people who use their martial arts skills to improve themselves, help their friends, be better family members and improve the world around them. Are you an Everyday Warrior? You can use the next section of the book to find out. Each of the next fourteen pages is about one of the qualities discussed by the Everyday Warriors in the first section of the book. If you look at the pages, you will see that they are mostly blank. That's because they haven't been written yet!

They are blank so you can write your own stories, just like the stories you have read so far. You don't have to fill them in all at once. Take your time. You might start now by filling in one page. First take a look at the page titles. Which one of the Everyday Warrior qualities have you demonstrated in your life? Have you been courteous to someone, did you use your martial arts skills to concentrate in a difficult situation? Did you show respect or self-control or perseverance? Think for a minute about what your story will be. How does it start? Where were you or what were you doing? When you write your story, don't forget to include how you felt at the time (scared, happy, sad, nervous, worried, excited) and why using your Everyday Warrior skills was important to you. Write as much or as little as you like, you won't be graded by anyone. You can even leave space in case you want to add another story later.

If you are too young to write a story, you can get an older person to help you. First, draw a picture of your story. It might be a picture of you helping someone or doing something that was hard. Leave some space underneath your picture. When you are done drawing or coloring, ask an older person to write down your story for you under your picture. That way, you will remember what your picture was about later!

Whenever you have some time or feel like it, fill in another page. Sometimes, you might do something at school or at home and suddenly realize that it would make a great story. That's a good time to write it down. Other times, you might have to think back to a time in the past. Sometimes you might not be able to think of anything at all. This could mean two things: you don't understand what the word means or you have never experienced this quality.

When this happens, go back and read the stories. For example, if you don't understand what empathy is, read the section on empathy again. Ask a grown up to tell you more about empathy or to explain the stories to you. You can even ask them for some hints on how you might show empathy in your own daily life. Once you understand the quality, make an effort to use it. Maybe your friend is really sad and you help him make a collage of pictures of his favorite to help him feel better. By looking for a chance to use your new knowledge, you helped your friend and you took one more step toward becoming an Everyday Warrior.

Filling in the pages that follow make take a long time, but that's okay. It's not a contest or homework or something that will be graded. It's a story about your life as an Everyday Warrior. When you read the stories in this book, you might have noticed that some people's stories cover many years. Even though the story takes only a few minutes to read, it took years to happen. Finding out about yourself and learning to be an Everyday Warrior can take a long time or a short time. You might find that some qualities you already have and some you have to work very hard at. That's perfectly normal. Everyone feels that way, even adults. Just stick with it. When you have completed all of the pages, we have a special reward for you!

Concentration

I demonstrated CONCENTRATION when I:

Courtesy

I demonstrated COURTESY when I:

Empathy

I demonstrated EMPATHY when I:

Perseverance

I demonstrated PERSEVERANCE when I:

Balance

I demonstrated BALANCE when I:

調
和

Honor

I demonstrated HONOR when I:

Humility

I demonstrated HUMILITY when I:

Indomitable Spirit

I demonstrated INDOMITABLE SPIRIT when I:

不屈

Integrity

I demonstrated INTEGRITY when I:

Justice

I demonstrated JUSTICE when I:

Respect

I demonstrated RESPECT when I:

Self-control

I demonstrated SELF-CONTROL when I:

Focus

I demonstrated FOCUS when I:

集中

Wisdom

I demonstrated WISDOM when I:

If this is a library book, please photocopy these pages.

Everyday Warrior

Certificate Application

When you have completed pages 94 through 107, you are eligible to become an official Everyday Warrior. Complete the front and back of this page, tear it out and send it to us. When we receive it, we will send you a personalized *Everyday Warrior Certificate*.

If you choose, you can also receive an Everyday Warrior patch to wear on your martial arts uniform.

Application Part One

Tell us about yourself so we can personalize your certificate:

Your Name _____

Mailing Address _____

City _____ State ____ Zip _____

Please print neatly or type your name address. This is the information we will use to personalize and mail your certificate.

Application Part Two

Ask your parent, guardian or instructor to sign below certifying that you have met the requirements:

I certify that _____ has completed pages 95 through 108 of the Everyday Warrior book and is eligible to be named an official Everyday Warrior.

Signature _____ Date _____

Application Part Three

If you would like to receive an **Everyday Warrior patch** for your martial arts uniform, please enclose $3.00 (check or money order) with this application and check below:

❑ Yes, I would like to receive a uniform patch with my certificate.

Important: complete part 4 on the back ⮕

Application Part 4

Below, please write or draw your favorite story from pages 94 through 107. If you like, you can photocopy your story or write it on a separate page and attach it.

If you give us permission, we might use your story in the next *Everyday Warriors* book or on the Everyday Warriors web site at www.turtlepress.com/warriors.htm. If you would like to be considered for this honor, ask your parent or guardian to sign below giving their permission.

I hereby give my permission for Turtle Press to publish my child's story above as part of the Everyday Warrior book and/or website. I understand that absolutely no personal information about my child will be divulged in connection with this story. Please list my child's name as _____ (first names only are acceptable).

Parent's signature _____ *Date* _____

Send this completed application to:

Everyday Warriors, Turtle Press, PO Box 290206, Wethersfield CT 06129-0206

Also Available from Turtle Press

Children's Books:

The Martial Arts Training Diary for Kids
A Part of the Ribbon: A Time Travel Adventure
The Kwon-dogs Learn New Tricks

For Parents:

Parents' Guide to Martial Arts

General Martial Arts Books:

The Martial Arts Training Diary
Teaching: The Way of the Master
Combat Strategy
The Art of Harmony
A Guide to Rape Awareness and Prevention
Total MindBody Training
1,001 Ways to Motivate Yourself and Others
Ultimate Fitness through Martial Arts
Weight Training for Martial Artists
100 Low Cost Marketing Ideas for the Martial Arts School
Herding the Ox
Neng Da: Super Punches
250 Ways to Make Classes Fun & Exciting
Martial Arts and the Law
Taekwondo Kyorugi: Olympic Style Sparring
Martial Arts for Women
Strike Like Lightning: Meditations on Nature
Martial Arts After 40

For more information or a free catalog:
Turtle Press
PO Box 290206
Wethersfield CT 06129-206
1-800-77-TURTL
e-mail: sales@turtlepress.com

http://www.turtlepress.com